EXIT Barney McGee

EXIT Barney McGee

Claire Mackay

COVER BY
LAURIE McGAW

Scholastic Canada Ltd.

Scholastic Canada Ltd.
123 Newkirk Road, Richmond Hill, Ontario, Canada L4C 3G5

Scholastic Inc.
730 Broadway, New York, NY 10003, USA

Ashton Scholastic Pty Limited
PO Box 579, Gosford, NSW 2250, Australia

Ashton Scholastic Limited
Private Bag 1, Penrose, Auckland, New Zealand

Scholastic Publications Ltd.
Villiers House, Clarendon Avenue, Leamington Spa, Warwickshire
CV32 5PR UK

Canadian Cataloguing in Publication Data

Mackay, Claire, 1930-
  Exit Barney McGee

ISBN 0-590-71863-0

I. Title.

PS8575.K27E95 1992   jC813'.54   C92-094170-2
PZ7.M32Ex 1992

6 5 4 3 2   Printed in Canada   2 3 4 5 6/9

*To all the Barneys
and all the Mikes.*

Contents

A painful decision

Even after a year of living under the same roof Barney couldn't call him "Dad." It stuck in his throat. Or it came out as "sir," or "Mr. Conrad." Or lately, nothing. In all his conversations with the man who had married his mother, an embarrassing blank space hung like a bad smell in the household air. Every sentence had a hole in it. So Barney made sure the sentences were few.

Besides, he wasn't at all sure he liked Mr. Conrad now. A year ago, as his grade six teacher, he had been great. Or at least okay. But as a father he was flunking out. He had changed in ways Barney couldn't understand — and didn't like.

Why had his mother married the guy anyway? Without Conrad they'd been fine, just the two of them. They'd managed okay as long as he could remember, his mom working at the library, Barney with his paper route and the delivery job at the drugstore. He remembered with regret the little apartment they used to live in over Parker's Furniture, right in the centre of Chessborough. Better than way out here in the boondocks, Barney thought for the fiftieth time, in this crummy falling-down old house that must've been built a hundred years ago.

1

That was the first lousy thing Conrad had done after the wedding. Zap! Inside of a week they were in the middle of nowhere, with Barney forced to take a bus home from school, forced to give up his jobs. His whole life was messed up. The only halfway decent part of it was the bush out back and the river curving through it to the deep black waters of Lake Neshika.

The second lousy thing, Barney reflected — and the anger which had smouldered for months somewhere in the centre of his stomach blazed afresh as he watched the VW pull into the driveway, as he watched them come towards the house smiling at each other — the second lousy thing was to get his mother pregnant.

And now here they were. The three of them, one brand-new. Barney opened the door.

"Hi, Mom!" His voice shook a little on the single syllable. He had missed her every day of the seven she had been in hospital, missed her badly. It was almost strange, seeing her again. He hung back.

"Don't you want to see your baby sister, Barney?" His mother's face was softer than he remembered. She looked sort of pretty, he thought. She seemed nearly as new as the baby, different somehow, as if some of the lines on her forehead and around her eyes had been rubbed off, the lines that had meant she didn't know how they were going to pay the hydro bill or if she could get him a good pair of skates for Christmas. He used to worry about the lines. He guessed now he wouldn't have to.

"Oh yeah, sure, Mom. You got a name for her yet?" He folded back a corner of the blanket that cocooned the baby and looked. Geez, what a mess! Uglier than a crocodile. No hair, eyes shut tight like scars, mouth open and twisted, no teeth. And then the thing let go a yell like the noon whistle down at the mill. Barney jumped.

"Isn't she beautiful, Barney? We're going to call her Sarah."

"That means 'princess,' Barney," chimed in Conrad. He was smiling all over his face, as if he'd had the baby all by himself, Barney thought sourly. And of course he'd know what the name meant — he always knew stuff like that. Princess. So that makes him a king. Instant royalty. Big deal. And what did that make Barney, then? The half-son, the half-brother. The outsider. It wasn't fair, Barney thought, it just wasn't fair. He turned away, trying to hide the sudden lonely feeling.

"Yeah, well, that's a great name. I really like it," he mumbled. And then, not knowing what to say, but knowing for sure he couldn't say the baby was ugly, he blurted, "Well, I'm sure glad you're home, Mom. I couldn't find my gym socks; you know, the ones with the green stripes. I looked all over and I can't find them any — " He stopped, feeling Conrad's eyes on him.

"Barnabas."

Oh-oh. Barney groaned inwardly. His name, uttered in that precise and sorrowful tone, was always the opening shot in a lecture he had

3

already heard too many times. He wished he could make himself deaf.

"I should think," the voice continued, "that you'd allow your mother to get inside the house and rest for a moment before you raise the matter of misplaced socks. You should take better care of your things, Barnabas. Remember, you're thirteen now."

"It's okay, Bill," his mother said quietly. "He just missed me, that's all." She sat down on the couch with a sigh.

Barney swallowed jerkily. "I'll — I'll make some tea for you, Mom. Okay?" He moved quickly to the kitchen and plugged in the kettle.

Slumped against the sink, Barney stared unseeingly at the scruffy grass in the backyard, whose roots showed white against the clumps of brown earth lately turned by Conrad's spade. A familiar melancholy enveloped him. Why, why was Conrad always leaning on him? "Act your age." "Grow up." "Be a man." The commands were like a recorded message, continuous and maddening.

"Be a man." Barney squirmed in rage. He *had* been a man, the only man around until Conrad had muscled in. And the worst insult of all was, "Why don't you help your mother?" He had helped for ten years, he thought, without anybody telling him to. Ever since his real father had gone away and never come back he had helped. Resentment rose in his throat and spread like a slow burning acid along his limbs, only to die in a futile tingle at the ends of his fingers and toes. He felt like smashing something.

His hands tightened on the edge of the counter. He didn't hear the kettle's rising whistle, nor see the steam misting the window, nor feel the spitting bubbles from the spout. He was unaware of everything until, behind him, he heard Conrad's voice.

"Great heavens, Barney! The kettle's boiling over!" Conrad seized the plug and yanked it free. "Where the devil's your head, boy?" He opened the cupboard door and reached for the Wedgwood teapot.

Barney grabbed it first. "I'll do it! I said I'd do it!" He clutched the pot to his chest. It was a special teapot. He had given it to his mother four years ago on her birthday. It had cost a lot — three months' paper route money. His mother's face had lit right up when she unwrapped it. They used it only on special days, celebration days like Christmas, or the last day of school, or when his mom got a raise, and once when Barney had won twenty-five dollars at a bingo game. And they used it too on bad days, to cheer themselves up: when the grey kitten was hit by a truck, when Barney had his bike swiped, when two guys had robbed him on collection night and he had limped home, his face wet with tears and blood. It was a special teapot. And Conrad had better not touch it.

"Now come on, Barney. Your mother's waiting for the tea." Conrad laughed a little and his arm stretched towards the pot. "Here, give it to me. You go find your socks instead."

Barney's eyes went wild. He lurched backwards and swung the pot away from Conrad's hand. It slammed against the stove. The spout snapped off and fell to the floor with a muffled clatter.

Barney looked at it. Then his glance flicked to his stepfather. "You made me do that!" His voice was thin, hissing. "It's your fault! That was Mom's birthday present! I gave it to her! And you made me break it!" His empty hand knobbed into a fist and he could feel the beating of his heart in his ears. "Why do you spoil things all the time?"

Conrad flinched and took a step backwards. His face was pale, his eyes wide and dark behind the horn-rimmed glasses. "Now, just a minute, son — "

"Don't call me 'son'!" The boy's taut whisper was louder than a scream. "I'm not your son! You're not my father! And nothing you can do will change that!"

Barney's voice trembled and gave way. He knew he was going to cry. He pushed blindly past the tall figure in front of him and ran out the back door.

* * *

It was no good. Just no good. It wasn't working out. It never would.

Barney watched the creek race towards Lake Neshika a kilometre north, watched it splash and tumble over its rocky bed. The sun glinted on its riffles, turning them into fringes of silver lace against the browner waters beneath.

The anger and the hurt were easing now. His tight muscles loosened and his breath smoothed and slowed. This place always helped. Strange, he thought, that it was Conrad who had shown it to him, back in the days before Mom had married him, when her name was still McGee. As Barney's was. It was Conrad who had shown him the nests of the water spiders, the hiding place of the green frog — *Rana Clamitans*, Conrad had called it, the Latin name suddenly surfacing in Barney's memory — the darting secrets of the fingerling speckled trout as they swam an intricate geometry in the darker, deeper, cooler pools below the wavering broom-like branches of the willows along the bank. It was Conrad who, on a dozen lazy Sundays, had sat here beside him while they had watched, motionless and entranced, the busy hidden life of the stream, the thrusts of a thousand tiny energies as they struggled, lost, survived. Barney had been happy those afternoons, glad that Bill Conrad was his companion. He had really liked the guy.

His face darkened abruptly. It was hard to believe it was the same Conrad who, for months now, had pushed Barney aside, had come between him and his mother. Barney had tried — how he had tried! — to understand. He had tried not to wince when his mother talked to Conrad instead of to him, when *Conrad* changed the light bulbs, when *Conrad* lit the fire in the fireplace, when *Conrad* put away the groceries in tidy alphabetical rows. He had tried even harder to mask his disappointment about Friday nights. He and his mom used to go to the movies on Friday night — it was payday for both of them. Not any more. Now she and Conrad played bridge — yeah, bridge! — with the vice-principal and his wife. Every Friday.

And Saturday nights, Barney remembered, they had played Monopoly, played it fiercely, laughing, out to win, making up their own rules as they went along. Once they had kept a game going for three months, arranging huge Rockefeller deals, grand piratical swaps full of daring and vision. It had finally ended, Barney recalled, in his brilliant master stroke: he had forced his mom to surrender the railways and utilities, her last pieces of property, to pay off a mortgage he had sold her. And in front of him had lain all the cash, all the real estate, and every house and hotel in the game.

His mouth thinned and hardened. It was no use going over the past. After Conrad moved in, there were no more movies, there was no Monopoly. After Conrad moved in, nothing was the same, everything changed. And Conrad was never going to move out. He had a kid of his own, brand-new. A wife who, as far as Barney could see, loved her husband more than her son.

It would have to be the other way, Barney thought, and something like fear, something like sadness, gripped him. He would have to move out.

But where could he go? He had no lonely aunts, no rich uncles looking for a nephew. His grandparents were long dead, buried and forgotten in a tiny village graveyard in Nova Scotia. He had no one but his mother.

And his father. His *real* father — not this stand-in who had messed everything up.

The boy's brown eyes narrowed in concentration. His memory of his father was dim and shifting, a picture fragmented and blurred. He couldn't separate what he truly remembered from the grudging bits and pieces his mother had doled out in answer to his little-boy questions. He dredged and sifted in his mind now for the chance remarks, the brief, clipped, almost cold responses that had dwindled as he grew older, as he grew into the knowledge that his mother felt pain when he prodded her for answers she couldn't give. Finally he had stopped asking.

Toronto. Wasn't it Toronto? Yes. His father had gone to Toronto. And wasn't there a letter somewhere? Barney snapped his fingers. He remembered now. The chest of drawers in his mother's room. It was the day they had moved. He had walked into her bedroom at the apartment and she had been standing in the middle of the room holding a thin packet of letters and papers in her hand, her eyes strange, looking at something that wasn't there, that was ten years away. Her face had been small and sad, the faint rosiness gone from under the skin. There must be something in those letters, something to tell him where his real father was.

Barney took a deep breath. Suddenly he shivered, although the sun still hung warm and yellow in the late afternoon sky. He got to his feet and stood for a moment, quiet, looking at the creek for what might be — what *must* be — the last time. He shivered again as he turned and walked away.

Picture from the past

"At last!"

Barney said the words aloud as the crunch of gravel signalled the departure of the VW. His mother and Conrad had finally left him alone after three long days, days filled with silences, with awkward courtesies, with constant pretending. They wouldn't be back for a while — they were going some place to show off the kid. As if she were a prize they'd won in a lottery.

He waited five minutes, then five more, in case they came back to collect a forgotten diaper, or bottle, or blanket, or any one of the million things Sarah seemed to need. Then he walked quickly to his mother's dresser, and as if afraid the walls might hear and report his espionage, eased the bottom drawer open. Carefully, not disturbing the folded, faintly scented clothes, the carved wooden jewel box, the bathing suit his mother might now once again squeeze into, the photograph album which held his own faithfully recorded history, he dug down underneath until his fingers closed on the remembered package. He pulled it out, closed the drawer and slipped into his own room.

Suddenly his legs began to tremble and he sat down on the bed. He stared at the packet in his hand. Right on top was a thick folded paper with the words *DECREE ABSOLUTE FOR DIVORCE* in big black print. He laid it aside. The envelope beneath was old, its edges thin and brownish. It bore a date of ten years ago and it was postmarked Toronto. Barney wiped his palms, cool with sweat, on the bedspread, then shook out the one-page letter.

He felt like a thief, a cheater. His face burned. In a painful flash he recalled an afternoon long ago in grade four when he had cheated in a social studies test, printing out the answers ahead of time on a tiny sheet of paper which he had taped to his wrist. The teacher had caught him. Worse than the zero, worse than the snickers of the kids, had been his mother's face when, eyes downcast, he had handed her the note from school. The scalding memory washed over him, and he felt once again his mother standing over him, her face pale and tight with disappointment.

He shook himself free of the image and scanned the letter. The scrawled message was short. *Dear Em,* it read, *Sorry babe, but I can't hack it. You're on your own. I'll send some cash if I ever get lucky. Forget the bad times and remember the good. Mick.*

Nothing else. No address, no date. Barney turned the letter over and peered closely at a few typewritten lines on the back. *OLYMPIA HOUSE — RULES FOR ROOMERS* was right at the top. Underneath was a set of blurred commands: *1. No radios after 11 p.m. 2. No pets. 3. No long distance calls from house phone without permission from landlady. 4. No guests after midnight. 5. Rent due every Friday. PLEASE PAY ON TIME.*

Barney sat for a moment, thinking. So, what did he know? He knew that ten years ago his father, Michael Dennis McGee, had stayed at a place called Olympia House in Toronto. Was he still there? Could Barney find him? His questions had no answers. But it was the only clue he had, and the only place he could start.

He refolded the letter and stuck it in his back pocket. He put the envelope back with the rest of the letters and was returning the package to his mother's drawer when a photograph, cracked, grainy, its edges bent, fluttered to the floor. He picked it up.

It was a man holding a baby. Barney turned it over. On the back, in faded ballpoint script, were the words *Mick with Barney at 13 months.*

Barney turned it face up again. His heart beat thick and hard against the bars of his ribs as he looked for the first time he could remember at the smiling young man who had held him so close twelve years ago. It was hard to make out his features. But Barney could see dark curly hair, like his own, falling into deep-set eyes, and a thin bony face grinning in a way that made you want to grin back. Something in the way he stood, feet planted wide apart, head on one side, hands square and firm and strong, reminded Barney of a pirate, or an outlaw, or a hero. His father looked lively and reckless and bold — all the things that Conrad wasn't.

Sure, maybe he didn't know that the Monarch butterfly sometimes flies at fifty kilometres an hour, or that the female praying mantis eats her husband for dinner; maybe he couldn't play bridge like an expert; maybe you couldn't set the clock by him — the way you could with Conrad. Maybe he just wasn't the kind of guy who could settle down.

But so what? Look at what he was! He was an adventurer, thought Barney, free of all the ordinary things, the dull routine stuff, the ruts of time and money. He had fled the road that Conrad had chosen, the narrow road to nowhere.

And Barney abruptly longed for what he saw in the photograph — the magic and the contrariness of his father's life. That way was the best! Just to walk into the unknown, take your chances, test your strength against the world — that was the best way! He wished they had known each other. They would have been friends, he knew. They would have had a ball. If only his father had not gone away! If only he had waited a while, given Barney a chance to grow up and be his friend, be the person who understood exactly how he felt!

The boy gazed at the picture for a long time, until he heard the humming *putt-putt* of the car as it rounded the corner of the driveway. Then, without a sound, he crept through the hall to his own room. He moved swiftly to the large aquarium under the window and began to sprinkle food on the water's surface, watching as the unmannerly fish below darted upwards in a riot of bubbles. He didn't turn when his stepfather knocked gently at the open door. At last, after the pause had reached the point of rudeness, he swivelled his head and said, "Yes?"

"Hi, Barney." Conrad's smile was uncertain. "Feeding the *Lebistes*?"

"You mean my guppies?" Barney's tone was cool. Darn show-off, he thought.

Conrad shifted from one foot to the other. "Uh, Barney." His fingers laced together, pressed against themselves, then unlaced. Barney suppressed a smirk. It was a habit of Conrad's he had mimicked many times. It never failed to get a laugh from the kids in science class.

Conrad continued to look at him, almost as if he were asking for something. After not looking at him at all ever since the teapot incident. Thinking of it once more, Barney's anger flared and his face set in a scowl.

"Barney," Conrad said again, "I — I picked up something I thought you might like." He went out into the hall and came back with a package. It was the size of a hat box, clumsily wrapped in brown paper. It made a faint squeaking noise.

Conrad cleared his throat. "Here," he said. "Open it."

Barney hesitated a moment, trying to stay aloof. Then, curious, he took the box and ripped it free of the paper.

It was not a box. It was a cage. And inside it, prancing on hind feet, was a mouse, a soft brown

15

and white mouse. With eyes bright as beads in the light of the afternoon sun, it regarded Barney unblinkingly.

"Oh, wow!" breathed Barney. A smile erased his harsh expression.

Conrad grinned. His body straightened as he said, "It's a Japanese waltzer, Barney. *Mus agitans japonicus.* Thought you could add him to your zoo. Do you like him?"

The boy turned to him, delight colouring his cheeks. "Sure thing! He's great! Thanks, Mr. Con—" Barney stopped, confused. Conrad's face changed, as if the shadow of a cloud had glided across a sunlit field. "I — I mean — well, thanks! I really do like him!"

Conrad's voice was flat and mechanical when he spoke again. "I'm glad. It is a token of my regret concerning the teapot incident." He turned and walked from the room.

Barney stood still, gazing at the stripes on his bedroom rug without seeing them. Whenever things didn't suit him Conrad would stiffen up and talk like a textbook. Barney felt all mixed up. What was the guy trying to do? Did he really feel bad about the teapot? Barney had trouble believing that. Conrad was probably just grandstanding, making a big show in front of Barney's mother maybe. And making Barney look like a crud! As if it were *his* fault the teapot got smashed! Or maybe Conrad figured he could *bribe* Barney into calling him Daddy every minute!

Barney's chin came up. No way! The lines were drawn. The decision was made. They didn't

16

want him. They didn't understand him. And he knew, he just knew, his real father would.

His glance fell on the tiny animal in front of him, its pink nose poking through the flimsy metal bars of the cage. The mouse tilted his head to one side, then drew back. He began to wash his whiskers with a swift composure, looking now and then at the boy on the other side of the bars.

Barney smiled and nodded slowly. He would go. The sooner the better. And the mouse would go with him.

Lies and goodbyes

Pulling the cord as tight as he dared, Barney moved the phone from the hall table into the living room. Through the transparent checkerboard of the leaded side windows he could see Conrad working in the garden, his body bent like a hinge. And that was another thing; every day the guy was out there, poking around, watering, pulling up weeds invisible to everybody else. And, like sentries in front of each flower and shrub, he had planted popsicle sticks labelled in Latin. Did it make a cedar grow faster when it was called *Cedrus deodara*? Was a daisy prettier with a name like *Bellis perennis*? Barney snorted with derision.

He listened for a moment. He could hear his mother singing somewhere in the back of the house. Sarah's bedroom. Good. He could make the call. He dialled slowly, letting his finger travel backward with each number, muffling the insect buzz of the release. After three rings Dave Nesbitt answered.

"Dave. It's Barney."

"Hi, Barn. What's happenin', man?"

"Tell you when I see you. I'll be at your place tomorrow at four. I want you to do something for me. Something important."

"Yeah? Sure, man, whatever you say, as long as I don't go to jail."

"Great."

The back of Barney's neck prickled. Behind him he heard a door open and close. Conrad, creeping up on him. He raised his voice.

"Hey, that'd be great, Dave. Yeah, sure I'd like to come. Just a sec till I check with Mom."

He pressed the receiver tight to his chest to silence Dave's bewildered sputter and yelled, "Hey, Mom, Dave wants me to sleep over tomorrow night. Okay?"

His mother shouted back. "Fine with me, Barney. Did he ask his parents?"

"Yeah, they said it's okay." Barney uncovered the phone and spoke rapidly. "Right, Dave. See you tomorrow at four o'clock."

He hung up in the middle of Dave's barrage of questions, hoping his friend would be smart enough to get the message. Then he turned, his face empty of everything but a smile.

Conrad had a strange look, puzzled, alert.

"Is everything all right, Barnabas? You seem . . . excited."

"Who, me? Everything's great. Gonna spend the weekend with Dave." He smiled again. "If that's okay with you?"

Conrad's eyebrows lifted in surprise, Barney noted with amusement. He could afford to be extra polite to Old Ramrod. His smile grew broader as he remembered the nickname the kids at school had given their upright science teacher. He could pretend to ask for permission. What a

19

laugh! One more day and he'd never see the guy again.

His heart leaped at the thought. It wasn't running *away*, he said to himself. It was running *to*. Running to freedom and new places. Running to his own father, who would, without endless words, half of them Latin, let him be what he was and should be. Yeah, he understood that last letter — his father couldn't be caged, locked in, tied down. Not like Conrad, who was in prison and didn't mind it a bit, and who was busy measuring Barney for the same kind of cell; not like Conrad, who would never comprehend that Mick and Barney McGee needed liberty and space the way ordinary people needed air.

* * *

The joy sustained him for twenty-four hours. Then came the tough part.

More than once during that time Barney asked himself if he were doing something really stupid. As he fed the salamander, the fish, the three turtles for the last time, reflecting that at least he wouldn't have to worry about them starving, not with a biologist right in the house; as he withdrew the $47.86 from his bank account; as he hid under the mattress the pajamas and slippers his mother had insisted on, replacing them in his knapsack with a heavy plaid shirt and jeans; as he stowed in his pants pockets enough sunflower seeds and crumbs of hard cheese to feed Saki for a day or two; as he did all these things, he had some bad moments.

Saki. The name, Barney remembered, had been Ramrod's idea, and grudgingly he conceded it was a pretty good choice. According to Conrad, saki was a strong Japanese wine, and when the mouse danced around in circles he really did look as if he were hammered out of his tiny skull. And Saki was also the pen name of a writer a long time ago whose stories, said Conrad, had a sly humour, the same kind of humour Barney could often see gleaming in the mouse's eyes. So the name fit, he thought. He was sort of surprised that Ramrod had come up with it. Sometimes the guy wasn't half bad.

In his times of doubt during that last day the same questions spun again and again in his head. What if his dad had moved? What if Barney couldn't find him? What if his dad had married someone else and had a whole gang of kids? What if his dad didn't want him?

Desperately, then, he would answer himself. If his dad had moved, he might have left a forwarding address. Barney would just keep asking till he found him. A man like his dad would be sure to have lots of friends — somebody, somewhere would know where he was. He would find him. He had to find him. And his dad would be glad to see him, he *would* want him. Barney was sure.

Then at last came the moment he dreaded. It was Saturday. The clock said half-past three. Barney stood at the kitchen door, his knapsack slung on his back.

"Well." His voice squeaked. Hastily he cleared his throat so hard it hurt. "Well, Mom, I'm — I guess I'm on my way."

His mouth shook suddenly, and he pressed his lips together. Keep it cool, he commanded himself. Pretend it really is just for the weekend.

His mother looked up from feeding Sarah. "All set, Barney?" She smiled at him, a full warm smile.

Barney's throat felt like sandpaper. He cleared it again. "Yep. Guess I got everything." His body seemed light, as if he had no bones. He crossed the room and kissed his mother on the cheek.

"So long, Mom," he mumbled as he straightened up. "Take care of yourself."

She looked at him quizzically and her voice was soft. "I've got someone to take care of me now, Barney, when you're not here. Remember?" She touched his face.

He moved back as if he'd been burned. The impulse to cry abruptly left him. His mouth tightened and the heat behind his eyes cooled and vanished. His voice was flat when he spoke.

"Yeah. That's right. Well, so long."

He was down the street and around the corner on his bike before he realized, with a fierce gladness, that he hadn't said goodbye to Conrad.

* * *

"Barn, you're crazy!"

Dave Nesbitt, skinny, hair the colour of straw, wrists and feet too big for the rest of him, scuffed savagely at the scanty gravel of the driveway beside his house. His face puckered in concern.

"Dave, I'd be crazy if I stayed!" Barney glanced at his friend, and once again his resolve faltered. He had forgotten somehow that he would be leaving Dave as well as Conrad — and the Mrs. Conrad his mother had turned into. He and Dave had been friends all their lives, even before they went to school. Dave had just always been around, as steady and sure as the air or the ground, part of the pattern of Barney's days and years. And now the pattern was breaking apart, shifting to one whose outline Barney couldn't guess, couldn't make out in the mist that had begun to cloud the future. But he knew one thing: Dave wouldn't be part of that future.

"Look," he said, his eyes dropping from Dave's face, "I've been over it and over it in my head. There's just no way I can stay there any more." His voice faded to a near whisper. "I've been over it and over it. It's been building up for a long time. They don't need me. I'm not even sure they want me now they've got Sarah." He was silent a moment, lifting his head and staring into the distance. "I think maybe my real father does need me." Dave strained to hear the last words. "And I'm sure I need him."

Barney's manner changed abruptly. "So it's settled, Dave." He fished in his pocket. "Here," he said, handing his friend a folded sheet of paper, "give this note to my mom when you take the bike back tomorrow night. So she won't worry.

And don't say anything to anybody till then. Okay?"

Dave stood without speaking, his face pinched and closed. His mouth was a straight sad line. Finally, with a reluctant hand, he took the note.

"But geez, Barn! What if your dad's moved? What if you can't find him? What if — something happens to you on the way?"

"Nothin's gonna happen. I can take care of myself okay. I've been doing it for ten years now. And so what if he has moved? I'll find him. He's gotta be somewhere. Don't worry, Dave. I'll be all right."

Dave let out a long, shaky sigh.

Barney glanced at him, then looked away. When the silence between them grew uncomfortable, he spoke. "You'll do what I asked you to, huh? I mean, I don't want my mom to get too upset."

Dave's voice was low. "Yeah, I promise, Barn." He lifted his head and looked his friend straight in the face, not caring if Barney saw the tears in his eyes.

"Aw, Dave, for godsake," said Barney softly. His tongue tasted like a blotter. He fidgeted with the straps on his pack. Then with a sudden movement he put his arms around Dave and the two of them stood there for a moment.

Barney stepped back. "See ya." He turned and hurried away towards the road that led out of town.

Dave Nesbitt watched the road for a long time, long after Barney had disappeared, not daring to move against the strange ache inside him.

* * *

Jumbled clouds, high and creamy, hung above the eastern horizon. They seemed pasted on the curved blue wall of sky behind them, like a child's cutout. The sun, yellow and warm and everywhere, spilled its afternoon light carelessly over rocks and trees and gleaming grassy hills. It was a great day. Barney's spirits lifted. As he turned onto the fourth concession road, he raised his face to the summer air and smiled.

"Well, Saki, we're on our way," he whispered, reaching up to touch the mouse inside the brim of his denim hat. "You okay? Come on down a minute and have a snack."

He curled his hand around the sleek small body and dug in his pocket for sunflower seeds. "There you go. How's that?" Grinning, he watched as the mouse extracted the seeds from their shells with surgical precision and placed them in his mouth. His tiny jaws worked like a miniature jackhammer, his pink nose probed the air, his eyes were vigilant and roving. Every muscle was tense with greed and caution.

Barney felt his own hunger stir. He unwrapped a stick of gum and folded it into his mouth. He knew his forty-seven dollars wouldn't go far, and he had resolved to eat only twice a day until he found his father. If he were lucky, that might be today. Once he reached the highway, he might get a ride all the way south to Toronto, about two hundred kilometres away.

He shifted the knapsack and unsnapped his jean jacket. It was getting hot. The pack seemed heavier. He began to sing under his breath, and moved his legs in the rhythm of the song. Two hundred kilometres was a long way. A long way. He walked on. The gravelled shoulder of the road moved slowly backwards under his plodding boots. The sun was a blast of heat at his back.

He reached the crest of a hill and paused. Some distance ahead of him the intersection of Concession 4 and the main highway sprawled in a huge untidy X across the farmland. Another hour, Barney said to himself, before he could start hitching. Couldn't risk it on this road. Might be somebody he knew. Glancing behind, he saw a moving cloud of dust and heard the faint hum of an approaching vehicle.

He moved off the road into the culvert and crouched down, hiding the red of his knapsack as much as he could. "Gotta hide, Saki. Nobody's gonna stop us now, right?" Saki crept quickly around the brim of Barney's hat, scratched once, and lay still. A rattling half-ton passed at Barney's eye level, the hubcaps a brief glint of clouded chrome. The gravel dust rose in a lopsided spiral and slowly fell to earth. The hum receded.

Barney vaulted out of the ditch and stood up. His jaw squared a little as he squinted after the truck. No. Nobody was going to stop him.

On the road

"Saki, let's take a rest."

Barney sighed. A good seven or eight kilometres south of the junction and no ride yet. Twenty-nine cars had whizzed by, ignoring his pleading thumb. And most of them were empty except for the driver. Miserable creeps!

His feet hurt. They were like swollen burning lumps on the ends of his legs. And his back ached. The knapsack's weight seemed to double every hour. Its straps sawed into his collarbones; he felt like a horse with a halter three sizes too small. Glumly he slouched over to the shade of a full-leafed maple and sat down.

He dug a couple of carrots out of the knapsack, stuck one in his mouth and with his jack-knife cut the other into small pieces, laying them out on a flat rock nearby.

"Hey, Saki, your supper's ready." He lowered the mouse onto the rock. Saki sat for a moment, his button eyes bright and wary, before he began his food ritual. He ran around the edge of the rock four times, then stood upright on his hind legs like a tiny ballet dancer. Moving forward, prancing slightly, he lowered his body elegantly to a morsel of carrot and gave it a connoisseur's sniff. As he did so the fine manners vanished:

single-minded, ravenous, yet with a meticulous grace, Saki chewed until the last crumb of vegetable had disappeared. Then the dance was repeated, and repeated once more. Barney laughed with pleasure. He never got tired of Saki's antics.

He gnawed on his own carrot, now and then glancing back down the road. Maybe the next car . . . maybe the next . . . If things didn't improve, he wouldn't get to Toronto until the middle of next week. He lay back on his knapsack and looked up at the sky. The east was shadowed now, with a stain of deeper blue spreading upwards from the horizon. He had to get a ride soon; with his dark jeans and jacket, to hitch at night was like asking to get run over.

The low whine of a motor alerted him. He sat up, struggling into the harness of the backpack. At the crest of the hill to the north a car appeared, then plunged down the long belt of asphalt towards him. Barney scrambled to his feet, tucked Saki into his hat and hurried to the edge of the highway. He stuck out his thumb.

The car slowed, slowed further, stopped. Zow! Barney ran to the door and yanked it open, a grin lighting his face. A woman, about his mother's age, smiled at him uncertainly. "Where are you going, young man?"

"Uh — Toronto, ma'am. Gonna visit my — uh — my uncle for a few days."

"Hmmm. Well, I only go as far as Linkford."

"Linkford's fine, ma'am, just fine! Anything's a help. I've been walking quite a while."

The woman glanced at him and then beyond to the descending sun. "Think you'll make it by dark? It's getting pretty late."

"Oh well, that's okay. I have some relatives in Stephensville. I can stay over with them."

There I go again, thought Barney. Another lie. He was getting good at it. One of the rules of the road, he guessed. A sudden sense of freedom enveloped him. For the first time he realized he could be anyone he wanted to be. Nobody knew him. He knew nobody. Nobody would ever know he was telling lies. He could choose his identity from a whole world full of people. Or make himself up, right out of his own head. He didn't have to be Barney McGee any more, son of Emily McGee. He shook his head impatiently — no, not McGee, not now. It was Conrad, Emily Conrad.

Sliding down in the seat, he cocked his hat forward against the sun — and Saki fell into his lap. Barney made a grab for him. He missed. Startled, or frightened, or obsessed with his own motion, Saki went into his jig right there on Barney's thigh. The boy glanced at the woman beside him. She was looking straight ahead, all unaware of the impromptu little circus act nearby.

Stealthily, by imperceptible degrees, Barney raised his left knee to shield the mouse from view. At the same time he took off his hat and held it ready. Then, as fast as he dared, he slammed it downwards. Gotcha! he thought.

But he was wrong. At the last moment Saki, luxuriating in freedom, interpreting the shadow and the movement of the hat as a threat, had leaped to the left.

He danced on the pink linen skirt for a full ten seconds before the lady looked down to determine the source of the dainty rhythmic tapping on her knee. Her scream set Barney's eardrums throbbing like a pulled bowstring, and rivalled the screech of hot rubber as she jammed on the brakes. The car shuddered, swivelled to the right and skidded along the shoulder to a lurching stop. Saki, alarmed at the noise and the unexpected jolt, scurried up the woman's arm and began to burrow into the bare flesh at the open neck of her blouse. And all the time the lady screamed.

"What is it? Get it off me! Help!"

Barney reached over and grabbed the only visible part of Saki, his tail, and pulled him loose. "It's only my mouse, ma'am."

"Only your mouse? Only your mouse?" The lady's voice climbed higher and then unbelievably higher until it was as shrill as a referee's whistle. "Out! Out! Get out of the car this minute! And take that — that — that beast with you!"

"Okay, okay," Barney mumbled. "Come on Saki." He pulled his knapsack from the rear seat. "Look, I'm sorry, lady. Really, though, he won't hurt you. He probably even likes you. He — "

The woman's voice, ragged and worn with screaming, was as cold as rain in November. "Get out of my car."

"Yes, ma'am." Barney clambered out and slammed the door. "Thanks for the ride!" He yelled the last words as the car fled down the highway and disappeared around a curve.

The boy looked into the bright eyes of the little creature in his hand. His words were a soft murmur. "Well, Saki, you sure got us into trouble." The mouse stared back at him, head tilted to one side, then ran up Barney's sleeve to perch on his shoulder.

Barney grinned. And as he remembered the look on the lady's face, the grin grew and grew.

* * *

"Thanks, mister."

Barney waved as the truck turned up the sideroad into the setting sun. He faced south again and started walking, almost mechanically now, his legs gone beyond fatigue into numbness. He felt like a robot. He had never imagined two hundred kilometres could be so far.

That last ride had sure helped though. Barney raised his eyes. *TORONTO 125*. The white figures stood out starkly on the deep green background of a nearby sign. Still a long way to go. It was getting too dark to hitch, and people might ask some tough questions. The cops might see him and wonder what the score was. No. He'd better start thinking of a place to sleep. And eat. He was hungry.

He pulled his money from his back pocket to count it again. Let's see, he had stopped for a plate of French fries and a milk shake. A buck and a quarter. Not worth it either. Then later he had bought a Coke at a gas station. Another thirty cents. Should still be over forty-five dollars left. In the dusk he riffled the thin wad of bills. Five, seven, eight, . . . he counted, barely deciphering the numbers as the last of the daylight slipped below the horizon. He heard a car, and turning, saw headlights enlarging in the dimness.

"What do you say, Saki?" Barney rubbed the soft belly of the mouse in his hat brim. "Shall we try one more?"

As the lights grew closer, Barney, not expecting success, idly raised his thumb. To his surprise the lights slowed and stopped. The car was a real oldie, a '64 Chev that had seen better days. And seen a heck of a lot worse too, Barney thought, judging by the rust-filled dents and gashes on its body. Shocks about gone too. The chassis almost scraped the ground in the rear. But at this point he couldn't afford to hold out for a Rolls-Royce. As long as the crate stayed glued together for a few kilometres, as long as it got him closer to Toronto, he'd take his chances.

The driver leaned across and pushed the door open. "Hi, kid. Need a lift?"

Barney smiled his thanks. He threw his pack in the rear and eased his stiff body onto the lumpy front seat. Unobtrusively he slid Saki into the breast pocket of his jacket and pressed the snap shut. Maybe this guy freaked out on mice too.

He glanced covertly at the driver. About seventeen or eighteen, he figured. The dim lights of the dash revealed a faint mist of beard on his cheeks and chin, a faded denim shirt, jeans that were worn and dirty. The guy was twitchy, Barney noted, strung-out, hyper. He kept looking into the rearview mirror, and his hand on the steering wheel showed white around the knuckles. A news broadcast came on the car radio and impatiently the young man jabbed at a button. Hard rock blasted into Barney's ears for a moment. Another jab, then silence.

"What's your name, kid?"

"Uh — Johnny. Johnny Smith. Goin' to Toronto to visit my uncle."

The older boy flashed him a look and his mouth curled. He glanced again into the mirror and drummed nervously on the wheel.

"Cut the crap, kid. Your name's not Johnny and you ain't gonna visit no uncle in T.O. You're runnin' away."

Barney's head snapped to the left as if he'd been struck, and his eyes widened in fright. "How'd you know?" he whispered.

The youth snorted with laughter. "It's written all over ya, kid." His eyes surveyed the boy. "Besides, I've run away plenty of times myself. I know the look." He fumbled above the dingy sun visor and pulled out a crumpled pack of cigarettes. "You smoke, kid?"

"No."

The older boy shook out a cigarette and lit it. "Just as well," he said disgustedly. "Last one." He took a deep drag, and the glow made sinister shadows of his eyes.

Ten minutes went by in silence. Then, so abruptly that Barney jumped, the older boy said,

"My name's Harry." He flicked the cigarette butt out through the no-draft. "So you're runnin' away, eh, kid?"

"Yeah." Barney shifted his body uneasily. Out of the corner of his eye he watched Harry's glance move from mirror to road in a crazy tennis match rhythm. What the heck was he so nervous about? Then he knew.

"You probably have some bread with you, right?"

Barney pretended he didn't understand. Fear tightened his stomach. He said nothing.

"Bread, gold, cash! Money, kid, money!"

"Oh. N-no, I only got a couple dollars. I figured on my uncle helping me . . ."

"Cut the crap, kid!" Harry said again. He reached into his pocket with his right hand. Barney watched, fascinated, almost in a trance, as the hand emerged with a knife. With a flick of his dirty thumbnail Harry pressed a release button. A blade flashed, like the silver tongue of a snake.

"Gimme the money, kid. I need it. All of it."

Escape from a nightmare

Barney's stomach cramped. Sweat, cold and oily, slid down the insides of his arms, surfaced on the skin of his thighs. He stole a look at the speedometer. It read fifty-two miles per hour — more than eighty kilometres. Outside, the hydro poles sailed through the dimming twilight at a reckless pace. No way he could get out of the car without killing himself.

As if he had read Barney's mind, Harry said, "Don't worry, kid. I'll let you out as soon as you hand over the money." He smiled. "Hey, man, no hassle, eh? Just hand it over. I'm runnin' away myself. From the cops. This car ain't mine, for one thing." He moved the knife closer until the shiny blade lightly touched the arm of Barney's jacket.

Scared, Barney pulled his arm away and huddled by the door. His voice trembled as he spoke. "I already told you, I only have a couple dollars. And I need the money myself!" The last word cracked as his voice rose in a thin piping cry.

Harry's answer came in a grating whisper, like metal on stone. "The money!" He flicked the knife downward. Barney felt a sudden fiery pain from his wrist to his knuckles. He looked at his hand as if it didn't belong to him. A narrow line of wetness, purple in the eerie light from the dash, sprang up from his skin, then welled into drops that ran together and spilled over the ridge of his bent fingers onto the cloth of his jeans.

"Okay! Okay, for godsake! What's wrong, you a nut or something? What're ya tryin' to do, kill me?" A sob of fear, mixed with a deep, deep anger, rose in the boy's throat. Dammit, he wasn't going to give this hood a cent if he could help it! A plan formed fuzzily in his mind. He had to stall for time.

"Slow down a bit. It's in my pack, right at the bottom. I'll have to take everything out." Barney half turned in the seat and the knife swung towards him again.

Harry's foot eased its pressure on the gas pedal as he said, "Get it. And no tricks, or you'll be missin' a finger." The car slowed further as he looked squarely at Barney. "I'm not foolin', kid. I got nothin' to lose. There's an old guy lyin' on the gravel at Linkford gas station who tried to get smart. He's still got his dough, but he won't be spendin' it for a while." Harry's jaw muscles bunched like a bag of marbles. "I gotta get away. And I need money to do it. Now hurry up!"

The white needle of the speedometer quivered at thirty, twenty-eight — and it was still dropping, Barney noted. He glanced down at Saki. A pink nose and a pair of bright black eyes showed at the corner of his pocket. Stay put, Saki, Barney said silently. Things may be a bit rough in the next few minutes.

He turned around in the front seat, kneeling, facing backwards. Leaning over the seat, he reached down with his left hand for the heavy backpack. His fingers brushed the metal frame as he fumbled for the straps.

"I said hurry up!"

"Okay, okay!"

Then Barney heaved, a roundhouse swing with all his strength behind it, and the pack flew forward. The right side of the frame, at the upper corner, slammed into the back of Harry's head. The youth shouted in pain and lurched forward against the steering wheel. The car veered sharply left, slewing sideways across the highway.

Barney, thrown against the door by the sudden swerve, was aware, as if from far away, of the handle smashing into his elbow, of the pain that sizzled like an electric shock along his nerves. He heard Harry scream a curse. And he saw the headlights probe the darkness and find only empty space, before the terrible sensation of falling overwhelmed him.

During that long moment as they fell, Barney, in a panic of despair, pressed forward on the door handle and pushed his whole body to the right. He felt a rush of air and flung himself out — down, down, down into blackness.

* * *

The moon sure is bright tonight, Barney mused. And right above me. Just as if I were outside. Woke me up.

He tried to raise himself to look at the clock on his night table. There was no table. There was

37

no clock. Pain made his eyes blur, made the breath stop in his chest. Then the memory of where he was and what had happened flooded over him.

He didn't want to move. He hurt everywhere. But questions, whispering questions that slithered through his mind like snakes, questions he knew he had to find answers to, forced him to move one leg, then the other. Then his arms — the good one, and finally the bad one. His elbow hurt the worst. Carefully he felt it with his left hand. Sore as heck, but not broken. He bent it slowly, experimentally.

Saki! His hand darted to his jacket pocket and flipped it open. A delicate squeaking, like the rustling of faraway leaves, reached his ears. With a sigh of relief and a rush of gratitude to something he couldn't name, Barney closed a trembling hand around the small silky body of his companion.

"Saki!" he cried, lifting the mouse free. "Are you okay, buddy?" With gentle fingertips the boy felt the tiny creature all over, remembering now what Conrad had taught him last year when they had studied mice at school, remembering where to touch along the fragile toothpick bones for fractures. He was thankful now for Conrad's patience, for his insistence that Barney learn these things. And when he recalled how he had made fun of Conrad behind his back, how he had dubbed him "The Whisker Frisker" who made "mouse calls," Barney was ashamed.

He got to his feet slowly, painfully, and leaned against a nearby tree for support. The August moon, not yet at its zenith, lit the landscape with a neon brilliance, dappling a river twenty metres below where Barney stood so that it seemed as if silver dollars skipped to and fro on the water's surface. The moonlight fell on the hood of a car whose headlights, pointing skywards, beamed a message in response.

A car! Barney felt his heart beat faster. Where was Harry? Swiftly he put Saki back into his pocket and made his way down the scrabbly hill to the shore of the river. The car must have bounced down the grade and rolled over a couple of times, Barney thought; its trunk was covered in water, its roof badly dented. It lay in midstream, four or five metres from where he stood. Dimly he made out the shape of Harry's head and shoulders bent over the steering wheel, strangely still. There was no movement, no sound except a soft sucking noise that for a moment Barney could not identify.

Then the car shifted in the water and seemed to settle deeper. It was sinking! A mixture of feelings tumbled through Barney as he stood unmoving on the riverbank. Let it sink, he said to himself. Let it sink! That creep'd be no loss to the human race!

The car moved again, its tires digging into the soft mud at the bottom of the river.

Barney dragged in a breath. His mind was a jumble. He wanted to run, to escape this nightmare place. But — there was Harry. He couldn't just leave Harry; he would drown for sure. If he wasn't already dead . . . Sure he was a crumb. He had swiped a car; he had hit an old guy up in Linkford; he had stabbed Barney, for godsake! But Barney couldn't just walk away from the river and leave him there. He couldn't.

Besides, in an odd sense he felt close to Harry, felt they shared something. They were both runaways, for one thing. Or throwaways, he thought, with a twist of bitterness. Maybe they were running from different things, but Barney guessed that deep inside Harry was lonely, as he was, and scared, as he was, and searching for a different kind of life, better than the one he had left behind. As Barney was. Yeah, they were the same in lots of ways.

Then fear touched him like a steel whip. Supposing he did rescue Harry? What then? What if he came to and pulled a knife again? The question ricocheted in Barney's mind until he recognized it for what it really was — a last shabby temptation to get out of doing what he must do. His body tightened with decision.

Abruptly the car shuddered. The dark skin of water closed over the handles of the rear doors. The back seat filled.

Barney ripped his laces loose and kicked off his boots. He waded into the muck at the edge of the river, sinking deeper with every step. Water lapped at his ankles, his shins. He moved farther out. Another metre, he thought. He took another step, pushing against the thick current, against the weight, heavier each second, of the black water. With a rolling spasm, the mud bed beneath him gave way. Panic raced through Barney for an instant until he found solid footing again. Water licked round his chest, almost up to the pocket where Saki lay, curled and quiet, one remaining spot of warmth. Barney's limbs felt sluggish with the cold. He reached forward clumsily and grabbed the right front door handle.

He could see Harry more clearly now. The youth's face, stark white in the surrounding darkness, looked like a Hallowe'en mask. It seemed disembodied, too large, unreal. A chill rippled through Barney's flesh, as if he had glimpsed something forbidden, something evil.

He shook his head and shut his eyes for a moment, forcing the fearful image from his consciousness. Furiously he wrenched at the handle, smooth and slippery and cold from the lapping river. Nothing happened. The door wouldn't budge, its latch bent and twisted from the plunge down the hill. With a noise like a sigh, the car sank farther into the muck.

"Open, dammit, open!" Barney's whisper was a half-sob. He could see the water slowly rising, filling the back seat to the misshapen roof, seeping into the tilted front, covering the floorboards like a deadly blanket. In the back, half submerged and out of his reach, floated his backpack, one corner slightly bent. Barney turned his eyes away, overcome for a sick instant with guilt and remembered fear.

He pulled again at the door. Nothing. Then, with a strength and recklessness he didn't recog-

41

nize as his own, he braced one foot against the drowning rear door. Ignoring the sudden sinking of the other leg as his balance shifted, he pulled at the front door with all his might. Slowly, with a muffled, watery creak, it came away from the body of the car. Barney pushed and pushed again, upward and out against a current that had seemed from the shore a mere sauntering flow, but that now had the weight and the catastrophic rush of a Niagara. Finally, reluctantly, the hinge went past the point of no return and the door hung open like an amphibious metal wing.

Barney's hat lay on the front seat beside Harry. He slapped it on his head with one swift motion and crawled in. Harry was very still. A trickle of blood ran from a cut above his right eye. The whole side of his face was purplish and swollen, eerily glazed with silver from the moon.

Barney hesitated. What if Harry's neck were broken? Maybe he shouldn't be moved. But the alternative was worse. If Barney left him to go for help, he would drown. The car sagged sickeningly under the extra weight of Barney's body, burying itself further in the riverbed. He'd have to take a chance. And right now.

He moved closer. Harry was breathing — Barney felt the faint warmth from the youth's partly-open mouth as he struggled to get a grip under his armpits. He pulled. Harry's head fell abruptly from the steering wheel onto Barney's arm. Barney pulled again. Geez, he was heavy! Then something caught. Barney looked down.

Harry's foot was jammed under the gas pedal, his leg twisted unnaturally. Easing the youth's body down on the seat, Barney reached around him and forced the foot free. Water sloshed and bubbled around it as it fell. Slowly, slowly, Barney edged Harry along the seat to the door. With a last tug, which sent a fiery pain along Barney's elbow and arm, he jerked the body free.

Both boys were now chest deep in water, Harry's slack weight half propped against the door frame, half leaning on Barney. Barney rested for a moment. His breath rasped like a file in his chest and throat. He felt as if he'd been standing in the river for a year, pulling and tugging at this stranger — this stranger who not an hour before had threatened him, had tried to rob him, had cut him with a knife.

Just then the car lurched again. A terrible vacuuming noise stirred in the depths below Barney's feet. The car sank another fifteen centimetres. Water rushed into the front seat where minutes earlier Harry had lain. The sudden downward thrust threw Barney off balance. Arms flailing, hat flying, he toppled backwards, and Harry fell after him into the swirling water.

Barney thrashed wildly, grasping at underwater reeds which broke in his hands. Finally, after agonized seconds, just as his lungs were about to explode, he fought his way to the surface. Harry's long blond hair lay like a shimmering net on the water. Barney grabbed it, and half crying, not afterwards knowing how he had done it, he dragged the limp body to shore and collapsed on the pebbly earth.

After a few minutes a faint but persistent chirp alerted him. Saki! Barney undid his pocket and hastily drew the creature out. Sitting on the boy's hand, Saki uttered a series of scolding staccato squeaks, then angrily licked his paws, already damp from the unexpected ducking. Rearing up on his hind legs, he whacked his whiskers in a ritual swipe, turned around three times and lay down.

A thin groan trembled in the darkness. Barney stepped to where Harry lay. Despite the terrible bruise, the youth's face looked like a sleeping child's, unwary, almost calm, with all traces of the violence and desperation washed away. Barney wasn't frightened of him now. And he couldn't be angry any more. Too much had happened there in the river.

He bent down. Harry's breath came in short, harsh whisperings. Barney felt for a pulse — the beat was strong and rapid. The flesh of his arm, the skin of his cheek were warm, too warm. Concussion? Skull fracture? Barney couldn't remember anything at all from the first-aid book he had once read. But he knew he had better get help. He straightened up.

Wearily, stumbling in the shadows, falling on his knees a dozen times, he made his way up the hill to the highway. About two hundred metres north there was a phone booth near a shuttered souvenir shop. Half-running, each plunging breath a needle in the cage of his chest, he

44

reached it in a minute. He dug a coin from his back pocket and as he did so, his mind registered the grim humour of the fact that he still had his money. If he'd handed it over, none of tonight would have happened. He dialled the operator and his voice shook a little as he gave the details of the accident.

"And what is your name, please?" Each syllable was memorized, Barney thought. Like a machine — or like Conrad on a bad day.

He hung up.

Once, as he cut west across the wooded fields to find a place to sleep, he looked back. The moonlight fell on a metal sign, etching in silver the name of a place he would never forget: Peaceful Creek.

A friend in need

"I'll have a hamburger without onions, a cheese sandwich and a chocolate milk shake, please," Barney said. "To go."

He pulled a couple of bills from the rumpled wad in his back pocket and smoothed out some of the wrinkles. They were still damp. The queen looks about a hundred and twenty and as messy as me, Barney thought; her crown's probably rusted right through. Earlier, when he had wakened to a brilliant sun already high in the sky, Barney had tried to dry his clothes and clean himself up, but a glance in the mirror behind the restaurant counter told him he hadn't done such a good job.

His body felt like stiff cardboard. The muscles in his arms and legs were stretched and sore, and his elbow was a swollen, bruised reminder of that reckless leap. Wonder if they pulled the car out of the river yet, he mused. Wonder if they found my backpack. Probably not. It was likely lying in the mud at the bottom of the river. Wonder how Harry is. Maybe he'll be okay. We weren't going too fast by the time we left the highway. Be a long time before he runs away again, though. Wonder what happened to make a guy act like that. Maybe things at home were bad, really bad. Like with me.

Suddenly, unbidden and unwelcome, the vision of his mother's face appeared before him. Homesickness overwhelmed him and his eyes blurred.

"Hey, kid! You deaf or just stupid?" The counterman's voice jarred Barney back to the reality of the third-rate, grease-encrusted café. "Dintya hear me? That's two-sixty. You got the money?"

Barney thought of a smart answer but decided he'd better keep his mouth shut. No sense drawing attention to himself. He didn't want trouble. No more than he'd already had. So far the trip hadn't exactly been full of fun.

"Yeah, I got the money. I'll take a Mars bar too."

"Last of the big spenders, huh?"

Barney smiled, to hide his anger, picked up his change and strode through the door into the sunlight. "What a creep! Hope he gets food poisoning. Come on, Saki, let's eat. I'm starving. Bet you are too."

Keeping away from the highway, Barney walked south a few hundred metres until, through a thick line of poplars, he spotted a cool-looking glen. He cut through the trees and within minutes had found the place for his picnic lunch. It was near the bank of a river — probably a feeder stream of Peaceful Creek, Barney thought, smiling once more at the name. To his right an old oak sheltered him from curious eyes; to his left, a huge flat stone jutted up from the earth, as big as a kitchen table.

Butterflies danced in the gentle air. He identified, almost in spite of himself, several monarchs, a group of yellow-margined mourning cloaks, and a few big black swallowtails. He shook his head, amazed that he still remembered what Conrad had taught him. The mourning cloaks were playing an intricate game of tag with a squadron of bumblebees near some red clover. As they swung and hovered, hovered and swung, the blue dots on their hind wings blinked like eyes. Barney watched them for a few moments, the afternoon sun warm on his face. A slow peace spread through him. He could feel his muscles, still ragged and bunched from the night before, begin to ease and soften.

"Okay, Saki," he murmured, setting the mouse on the flat rock. "It's chow time." He unwrapped the food and broke up half the cheese sandwich for his companion. The little mouse quivered with excitement, then approached the food and paused theatrically. He stood on his hind legs, toes arched like a bird's feet for balance, forelegs folded over one another as if he were wearing a kimono. Only after he had bowed towards Barney and skipped through a short waltz did he advance to his banquet and eat. Barney laughed through a mouthful of hamburger.

The last of the milk shake gurgled through the straw. Sighing contentedly, Barney lay back and gazed at the brilliant sky. Above him, far, far above, a hawk hung lazily in the air, riding a thermal, its broad wings set and still. Barney squinted, trying to identify it. The bird veered in its flight for a moment and Barney glimpsed a flash of brick-coloured feathers. It was a red-tail. He watched, fascinated, as the hawk soared, settled, swooped in the upper air. Wouldn't that be great, he thought. Man, that was freedom! Nobody to bug you up there.

A noisy splashing abruptly banished his daydream. He sat up, every sense alert, then crept to the edge of the riverbank. About ten metres downstream, in hip-high waders, net in one hand, spinning rod bent double in the other, stood a woman, her small sturdy body braced against the current as she fought a big fish. Grey hair, curly and untidy, sprang out from under a battered baseball cap cluttered with lures. Barney slowly shook his head in wonder. She was quite a sight. Then his wariness surfaced. He'd better get out of there. The fewer people, the fewer questions.

He scurried backwards from his perch. Gathering up the foil wrappings and the grease-stained paper bag, he crammed them into a tight ball, and after digging a shallow hole with his boot, buried them behind the big oak. The burning sun lay flat and malignant in the western sky. Briefly he wished for his lost hat.

"Come on, Saki, time to go!" he whispered.

Suddenly a huge and dreadful flapping filled the shadowed air around Barney's head. Instinctively he threw up his arms. His attacker veered. In a blur Barney saw a belly barred with black and white, a sharp beak, curved and wavy on its upper side, and the rusty tail feathers of the hawk he had lately envied. It was after Saki!

Barney lunged forward and grabbed the mouse just as the bird, now as startled as the boy, swooped erratically, its rasping cry a sound beyond the real and beyond the imaginable. He felt the talons scrape at his knuckles as he tried to shield the mouse. He cried out in pain and fright, running towards the river in confusion. The chunky wings, smelling of dryness, of dusty warmth, of blood, whipped at his ears, flailed at his eyes. His breath seemed sucked from his chest by a cloud of rigid, battering feathers. But he kept his fist right around Saki. His fingers felt the shiver of the mouse's heart against the fragile ribs, the shake of terror in the fur.

Robbed of sight, Barney failed to glimpse the mossy boulder hidden on the riverbank three metres above the water. His boot struck its angled side and he skidded, losing his balance. As he sprawled forward and rolled down to the pebbly shore, Saki flew from his hand. Dimly Barney heard a whistling swish, a shout, and the terrible grating scream of the bird, a slurred, descending "Keeer-r-r!" The angry thrum of wings grew fainter and fainter and faded to silence. Wonderful silence. Then slowly to Barney's clearing consciousness there came the gentle river sounds, the humming counterpoint of insects from the field beyond — and the squeaky crunch of rubber boots on gravel. He looked up.

The fisherwoman stood above him, smiling a little. "Hi," she said. "This fellow belong to you?"

She bent forward and offered Barney her baseball cap.

Barney struggled to a sitting position, and stupid with shock, stared first at her, then at the cap, then back at her again. She laughed, a deep contralto which rumbled and cracked in the quiet air. "Only thing I caught all day and it's not even a keeper. Here." Once again she offered the cap. Barney looked inside to see Saki curled in the bottom, nose twitching in bewilderment. He reached convulsively for the tiny animal and tucked him into his jacket pocket. "H-how did you . . . ?"

"Easy. Scared off the hawk with my net. Saw your pal there heading for the trees so I pitched my hat over him. Hey, let's have a look at your hand."

Swiftly the woman knelt beside him and pulled a first-aid kit out of her windbreaker pocket. As if she had done it many times before, she swabbed some cream on the red furrow left by the hawk, laid a strip of gauze over it, ripped adhesive tape from a roll and slapped it firmly across his knuckles. "There. That should fix it."

With a grunt the woman got to her feet. "Better hide that mouse of yours from now on." She grinned down at Barney.

It made her face light up like a sun, Barney thought, and found himself grinning back. With an effort he finally made his tongue work. "Gee, thanks, ma'am. I don't know what I would've done if you hadn't been here. I guess I would've lost Saki for sure. I'm just glad you were around." The words came out in a rush.

The woman waved him to silence. "Forget it. High point of my day." She put on her cap and turned to go, hesitated, then turned back with a sigh. She looked at the boy for a minute. A runaway. She sighed again.

She had seen so many of them in the last thirty years. Thirty years of trying to help kids, of trying to help parents help their kids. Thirty years of kids from broken homes, kids in jail, in hospitals, kids so spaced-out on drugs they were less than robots, desperate kids with too much money or too little. She had rescued some, shown others how to rescue themselves. But not many, not enough.

Her mind cringed in familiar anguish as she remembered one she hadn't been able to help, one who had fled from her ten years before. She hadn't even known where he was until the Vancouver police had called last December. They had told her it was an overdose and had shipped the body home in time for Christmas. Three days later she had stood in a cemetery north of Toronto and had watched them bury her son beside the father he had barely known. Something had happened to her then, something that wouldn't go away. Since then she had felt empty and worn down and remote from everybody, including herself.

Then why, she asked silently, was she still standing here with this kid? Suddenly she heard her own voice asking, "You going any place in particular?"

"Uh, I'm going to Toronto, ma'am. To visit my uncle."

Omigod, she thought, can't he do better than that? But she kept her face expressionless and said aloud, "It's a long walk. Care for a lift?"

Barney searched the warm round face, seamed with wrinkles near the eyes, but marked too with a sorrow he couldn't guess at. She looked okay. She didn't ask questions. She wasn't scared of fish-hooks, hawks or, he reflected, mice. It was the last that made up his mind.

"Yes, ma'am, I sure would!"

"Come on then. Got my jeep on the side road." She plunged ahead, heedless of the burrs and thorns that clutched at her windbreaker. As they reached the battered, ancient jeep she turned her head and said, "My name's Nell." She grinned and whispered, "It's really Cornelia, but don't tell anybody. What's yours?"

Barney hesitated, but only for an instant. "Barney," he answered. "It's really Barnabas — and don't *you* tell anybody."

Smiling, Nell pushed the gas pedal and they took off with a bone-throbbing roar.

The big city

"Hold it, Bert!" Eddie, the owner of the garage, shouted and waved his arms in an excited negative. "Okay, now let 'er down slow!" He motioned the flashing tow truck nearer. "Forward a bit — you're blockin' the pumps. Okay, easy, e-e-easy! Fine, Bert, she's down!"

The wreck of what was once a 1964 Chev sank exhausted on the haunches of its ruined springs. The roof and sides looked as if they had been through an artillery barrage. Out of the front doors, hanging on their hinges like twisted cardboard, water leaked in a steady dripping from the soaked upholstery. The hood, forced upward, gaped crookedly.

Bert, in grease-smeared jeans and T-shirt, hoisted his skinny frame from the cab of the truck and jumped to the ground beside his boss. They stood on the hot asphalt apron a few moments, silent, appraising the day's catch.

Eddie whistled under his breath and lit a cigarette. "Still don't know how the kid got outa that without killin' himself. It shoulda been his coffin. Can't figure how he got to shore. Musta had somebody" — Eddie jerked a thumb heavenwards — "lookin' out for him." He shifted the cigarette from one side of his mouth to the other, keeping the long ash intact, and shook his head in wonder. "Beats me. Well, best leave it as is till Sergeant Vanderlinden comes round tomorrow. Said he wanted to have a look at it." He shrugged. "Sure not much good now, not even for scrap." He turned away as a van pulled in for gas.

Bert stood for a minute contemplating the wreck. It was a shame to see a car in that shape. He walked around it slowly. Body was bad, but still . . . He sure wanted a car. It was one of the reasons he'd got the job with Eddie. He had a couple hundred saved already.

He surveyed the Chevy again. Parts of it might be okay. Tried the doors. The rear ones seemed to be all right. He opened the right rear to try the window and a patch of red caught his eye, sticking out from under the front seat on the floor. He bent over and pulled. It was a cloth bag of some sort. He yanked again. Must be caught on a loose spring. He reached in under the front seat and felt around for the snag.

"Ow!" His thumb collided with the end of the coiled spring. But the bag came loose and he pulled it out of the car. A knapsack. Probably belonged to the guy who was now unconscious in the hospital. But Eddie had said it was a stolen car. Maybe the pack was the owner's. Bert undid the soggy strap and opened the top flap. A name tag was sewn neatly in place: *B. McGee, Chessborough, Ont.*

"Hey, Eddie," the young man called, "look what I found!"

* * *

A hundred and twenty kilometres north, a low red sun sat tentatively on the horizon. Its long beams slid through the kitchen window of an old house not far from Chessborough, filling the room with rosy light.

Emily Conrad stood at the counter, motionless, thoughtful. The watering can she held in one hand had long since finished its task of sprinkling the African violets, all neatly labelled in Latin. The place was so *quiet*, she mused. With only Bill and Sarah around, it had been almost — well, lonely. A twinge of guilt touched her briefly. How could she be lonely with Bill and the baby? Weren't they enough?

But she had missed Barney, really missed him. It was strange without him. He had been there beside her for so many years, for all of his life and a third of hers; he had been part of her day, part of her night, part of her present and her past, and until last year she had thought he would be most of her future. She couldn't imagine a time without him.

Well, it shouldn't be long now. She smiled. It was nearly dark. He would be home any minute.

Her face lost its smile momentarily. If only Bill could be more understanding, she thought. And if only Barney could unbend a little, could give up some of that fierce independence of his. Of course, she had helped to make him that way, she knew; after Mike had gone away, she had had no choice. And up to now she had always been glad of Barney's self-reliance, glad that he could think for himself and make his own decisions.

But now she wasn't so sure. Even in the midst of her own new happiness in the last months, she hadn't been able to ignore the growing friction between her husband and her son. Most of the time they circled each other suspiciously, like two dogs meeting on a street corner. It almost seemed that Bill, once married, had resolved to turn himself into a proper father overnight. The trouble was that his idea of a father wasn't hers, wasn't anybody's anymore: his sternness and his discipline were right out of the nineteenth century. He had forgotten, as if it had never happened, all the fun, all the laughter and friendship which he and Barney had earlier shared. She had hoped Sarah might make a difference, that once Bill had his own child he would soften a little towards Barney, would throw away the old-fashioned rule book he seemed to be following. But so far it hadn't worked out that way. Emily sighed. Give them time, she thought. Give them time.

The creak of a step on the back porch roused her from her musings. That would be Barney now. Swiftly she moved to the door and swung it wide, a smile of welcome ready on her face.

In front of her, looking scared and uncomfortable, stood Dave Nesbitt. His hand trembled as he held out a piece of paper. Before she could say a word, before the fear began to make her knees shake, the boy ducked his head to avoid her eyes and said, "Mrs. McGee — uh, I mean Mrs. Conrad — Barney asked me to give you this."

* * *

Nell's laugh boomed out over the deserted picnic area. It was full and round and irresistible, and from a woman barely as tall as he was, astonishing. A laugh should always sound like that, Barney thought, hearing his own chuckle as a puny echo.

"He's a terrific performer, Barney." Nell shook her short grey curls in admiration. "Here, Saki." She scraped together some leftover bits of the fried chicken they had just eaten and offered them to the mouse. Saki executed a final twirl, poised for a moment on his hind legs, then, with sharpshooter precision, polished off every crumb.

Nell rose to her feet and stretched, her eyes squinting against the dying sunlight. "Well, let's go, Barney. It'll be dark soon. I'd like to hit the city before it gets too late."

They were in the jeep before she spoke again. "Why Saki?"

It took a few seconds for Barney to understand the question. "Oh," he said, "that was a name my — uh, my stepfather — " His throat locked on the word. It was a wicked word from a fairy tale, not from his own ordinary life. "My stepfather made it up." He explained how the name seemed to fit. "Neat, huh?"

"Yeah," said Nell, "quite neat." She glanced at her companion. "Sounds like an interesting guy, your stepfather."

The boy's face closed, the features hard and tight and pale. "Yeah. I guess."

58

Nell Weatherston nodded imperceptibly to herself. That was the trouble, then. She smiled a small, rueful smile. Right again, Cornelia, she whispered inwardly. Aloud she said nothing.

Fifteen kilometres of highway passed beneath the rugged tires before Barney said abruptly, "Yeah, he's pretty smart all right. Knows the right names for everything, always has everything sorted out. He likes things to be organized." And he added, so low that Nell strained to hear, "Even the people around him."

Barney clamped his mouth shut. What was he doing? Spilling his guts out to this strange woman he'd met only a couple of hours ago, giving himself away. Now she'd start the questions. He braced himself to lie.

The woman beside him said nothing. After a minute Barney sneaked a look at her in the dim light. She was as calm as Lake Neshika on a windless morning. Her face was the same as before, quiet, ready to laugh, untroubled. He was puzzled. Then the tension ebbed from his muscles and he silently gave her another gold star. She wasn't nosy.

The moon, a fat globe of tarnished light, rose through the poplars on a distant eastern hill. Nell rolled up her window and pulled the no-draft shut as the cooler night air blew into the jeep. Barney did the same.

"There's the big city," she murmured as they crested a shallow rise.

Barney sucked in his breath. A million lights lay before him, a twinkling carpet thrown by some giant hand to mock the Milky Way. From one side of the world to the other, the tiny lights, small points of human meaning in the darkness, blinked their messages to him, messages of welcome and promise. He wondered which light in that glorious maze belonged to his father, which light this very instant illuminated the merry face in the blurred photograph, kindled the eyes and mouth in a way that made Barney's memory stir, moved by something he knew, yet could not remember knowing.

They plunged into the city. Nell twined her way expertly through the snaking cloverleafs, turnoffs and service roads until they were racing along a highway as wide as an airfield. A huge green sign with glaring white letters announced *AVENUE RD. 3 km.* Nell edged into the lane beneath it.

She looked at the boy beside her and shook her head slightly before she asked, "Where can I let you off, Barney?"

Bewildered by the rushing darkness, the cars, the zigzagging network of roads, Barney couldn't answer. Panicky, he turned towards her. "Uh," he said, then stopped. He had almost blurted out "Olympia House." He cast about in his memory and came up with a name. "Oh, anywhere along Yonge Street will be fine."

Nell sighed. "Yonge Street runs the whole length of the city, Barney." Then she relented. "How about Yonge and Bloor? That's the centre of town." She smiled at him. "You can find your way any place from there."

Barney smiled back, grateful that she said no more, that she wasn't going to grill him. "Yeah, that'd be great, Nell. Yonge and Bloor sounds fine."

They rode in silence for another few minutes. The traffic thickened, clotted with slow-moving cars as they crawled past the city limits and south to the tallest buildings Barney had ever seen. He started to feel small. And scared. He had forgotten how big Toronto was. All the people in Chessborough could probably fit in one building, he thought. One good thing, though — it would be easy to disappear. With the thousands of people he saw hurrying along the sidewalks, lining up for movies, pouring across the intersections, it would be hard to find a thirteen-year-old boy who didn't want to be found.

Finally Nell slowed and pulled over to the curb. Ahead of them, on a stark grey building that looked like a prison, Barney could see enormous yellow letters that spelled out *The Bay*. Nell put the jeep in neutral and set the emergency brake. She turned in the seat and looked at Barney for a moment, then asked him softly, "Barney, are you going to be okay?"

The boy was instantly on guard. "Sure."

Nell chewed briefly at her lower lip and dropped her gaze. She pulled a card from above the visor. "Well, we all have to find our own way, Barney. You, me — even your stepfather. But sometimes some of us can use a little help." She passed him the card and in the shadowy glow of the streetlight nearby he read her name and telephone number. "if you need a hand any time, give me a call."

Barney's eyes blurred. He lowered his face so she wouldn't see, and fumbled for the door handle. As he opened the door he felt her warm fingers on his cheek.

"So long, Barney."

"See ya, Nell." He gave her a shaky smile, waved and stepped out into the city.

A grim message

"What's the name again, Eddie?"

Sergeant Vanderlinden, the phone hugged to his ear with one meaty shoulder, reached for his notebook and flipped backwards to last night's accident report.

The gravelly voice of the garage owner came slowly over the wire as he repeated the name. "Tag says 'B. McGee, Chessborough, Ont.,' sarge. That the name of the boy in the wreck?"

"Nope. At least it's not the name we found in his wallet. Driver's licence says Harold Moss. And the car belonged to a fellow in Linkford named Spivak."

"Maybe the Moss kid swiped the knapsack?" Eddie's voice rose questioningly.

"Could be. We won't know till he comes to. He's still out cold, according to the hospital. They're shipping him down to Toronto for some more tests."

Eddie made clucking noises at the other end. "Still a puzzle to me how he got outa that wreck. Is he hurt bad?"

Vanderlinden moved the phone to his other ear and reached for his coffee. He put it to his mouth, then made a face. It was black and sugarless. For a moment he had forgotten his diet and the police doctor who had strongly suggested it last week. He felt insulted. He wasn't fat. Maybe a little heavier than he used to be, but all the Vanderlindens were big. And now his wife was slowly starving him to death! He downed the coffee in one quick gulp to shorten the agony.

"Don't know. Doctor at Benedict says a bad concussion, cracked ribs, head wound. Sleeping rough the clock." Vanderlinden snorted suddenly, and the roll above his belt writhed like a snake. "Poor guy's got nothing much to wake up for, Eddie. Armed robbery, assault, car theft. That's what's waiting for him."

Eddie clucked again. "That so? Too bad. Just a kid, ain't he?"

"Yeah. Seventeen. He's from up Linkford way — I was through to the detachment up there. Had a crappy life so far. Father died when he was a kid, mother disappeared out west someplace. He was taken in by a couple of no-good uncles who worked him harder than a mule and belted him for kicks." Vanderlinden shook his big head in disgust. "The kid's never done anything like this before, though. He ran away a few times is all, and I can't say I blame him. Judge might go easy on him." He shifted his bulk and the chair creaked threateningly. "Anyhow, Eddie, you hang on to that pack and I'll get it tomorrow on my way to Toronto. Meantime I'll phone Chessborough and see what they know."

"Okay, sarge, I'll do that. See you tomorrow."

The phone clicked in Vanderlinden's ear. He leaned back, stretched, rubbed his stomach slowly and tenderly. Lord, he was hungry! He rooted around in his lunchbox and found a small foil-wrapped package. Eagerly he unfolded it. Celery. Celery! Pushing furiously away from his desk, he slammed on his cap and strode across the street to the Donut Shop. He growled forbiddingly at the young girl behind the counter. "Gimme two chocolate eclairs and two jelly doughnuts to go. And a coffee. Double sugar, double cream."

Unsmiling, furtive, he stepped out of the shop into the darkening street and walked quickly back to the office. Then carefully, almost reverently, he spread the food out in front of him on the green blotter that covered his massive and untidy desk. A sigh of contentment escaped him. He reached for the phone.

In a moment he was through to Chessborough. "Sergeant Vanderlinden of Benedict here." Rapidly he sketched in the details of the accident to the listening constable.

"Okay, sergeant, we'll check it out and get back to you. Only a few McGees around here. Ten-four."

Vanderlinden's answering "ten-four" was unintelligible as his mouth closed over the first doughnut. Hell with it. Tomorrow. He'd go on a diet tomorrow.

* * *

Emily Conrad read the note again. The words danced foolishly in front of her eyes; each time she looked at the neatly pencilled message it made less sense. The paper, torn from one of

Barney's school notebooks, was wrinkled now, some of the words faded, so often had she unfolded and refolded the little white square.

"Dear Mom . . . " She knew it by heart, but she made her eyes follow the words again, hoping to find more, hoping to discover some meaning there that would make it hurt less. "Have gone away by myself for a while. Will write you a letter later on. Don't worry about me, I'll be okay. Love, Barney. P.S. I took Saki with me."

Bill had pried a little more out of Dave, although the boy was scared and reluctant. Imagine, Emily thought, Barney going to find his father! After all these years! Why would he want to do such a thing?

"Who knows?" Bill's voice answered her, and with a start Emily realized she had spoken aloud. She glanced at him. He looked pale; he was blaming himself, she knew. She reached out and laid her hand over his. He smiled at her bleakly, but his voice was firm when he spoke. "Well, first we have to find out where he went, Emily. Do you remember where Mike was living the last time you heard from him?"

"In Toronto some place, Bill. I'm not sure where." She sat up suddenly. "Wait a sec." She moved towards the bedroom. "I kept his cards and letters, the few he sent." Her face was cold for an instant; then the look was gone. She was back in a moment with a slim packet. "I know it's here somewhere." Her fingers riffled through the bundle. She frowned.

"The letter's gone, Bill! The envelope's empty!" Her voice shook a little. "It was from Toronto, about ten years ago. He was at some hotel. It was the letter that said he wasn't coming back."

Bill Conrad moved to put his arm around her shoulders. "I think I know where it is. I think Barney took it."

Her hands stopped and fell into her lap like captured birds. "Yes," she whispered, "of course." She was silent a moment, her grey eyes staring at nothing. Then she leaned limply against her husband's arm. "We'd better call the police."

"Yes." Conrad stood up and strode to the phone, but just as his hand reached out for it, it rang. The sound startled him into immobility. He looked at the instrument stupidly. It rang again, impersonal, insistent. He heard Emily come into the hall to stand behind him. The phone shrilled once again. He picked it up with convulsive fingers.

"Hello."

"Hello. Constable Martindale speaking. Is this Mr. Conrad?"

"Yes." He could feel Emily's fingers tightening on his arm.

"Mr. Conrad, we had a call from the Benedict police. They found a knapsack, red nylon, with the name B. McGee sewn inside the flap. Chessborough was the address. And the only B. McGee I could think of is your stepson."

Bill Conrad's knuckles were white against the black receiver. "Go on, officer."

"Well, sir, is your boy at home?"

The words rattled around in Conrad's head: "your boy . . . your boy . . ." It was a minute before he could reply. "No, constable. Barney's not here. Where did you say the knapsack was found?" He could hear Emily's quick surge of breath, feel her body go tense against him.

"Well, Mr. Conrad, I don't want to alarm you, but it was found in a car pulled out of Peaceful Creek this morning, a couple of kilometres north of Benedict."

"I see," said Conrad, and for a detached split second, wondered at the absurdity of the human mind. In this moment of crisis, at this peak of anxiety, all he could summon from his remarkable vocabulary were two idiotic monosyllables. "As it happens, officer, we were just about to call you. Barney's left home. He told us he was spending the weekend with a friend. We last saw him yesterday afternoon." He fell silent as the policeman mutteringly made notes. "Perhaps I should come to the station? Or will you come here?"

"I'll come over, Mr. Conrad. We'll need a picture, description, notes on what he was wearing, identifying marks, things like that. I'll be there in ten minutes."

"All right. That will be fine." Again he wondered at his calm formality. As if he were making a dentist appointment or ordering a roast of beef. Then carefully, quietly, with his habitual precision of movement magnified by the beginnings of shock, he replaced the receiver and turned to face Emily.

His tongue formed the words against his will. "The police found Barney's pack in a river near Benedict. It was in a car wreck. But there's no sign of — of him." Conrad had almost said "his body" but swerved from the phrase in time, only to realize that it hung in the air between them, louder and more terrible because unspoken. He flinched as he watched Emily's eyes change and go flat.

Olympia House

Barney stood in the doorway of a men's shop and pretended to look at the ties and socks. He had never imagined there could be so many people in one place. He stared at them as they passed in front of him, singly, in pairs, in groups of three and four, a flamboyant and formless parade that never stopped moving. And never stopped talking either, thought Barney, as he gazed in fascination at mouth after open mouth, all working away making sounds, feeding the din which surrounded him. He felt bombarded, battered with noise: the hiss and groan of airbrakes; the horns that quacked indignantly like angry ducks; a siren, far away; a shouted chorus of blues, in stereo, from an open window half a block west; the muted grumble of the subway under his feet; and a hundred, a thousand, a million conversations.

Barney had a sudden sharp sense of being alone, of being alien, as if he had dropped by mistake into another world. Everything was different from the reality he knew, from the order and the quiet and the expectedness of Chessborough where people said comforting, straightforward, familiar things to one another, where people smiled and walked with solid steps and moved and lived in patterns and rhythms Barney understood. Everything was different. And all the people were different; they were strangers to him, really strangers, as if they belonged to another species.

He crossed the street, borne along by the crowd as the light changed. Once on the other side, he took a deep breath to steady his nerves. His stomach plunged in alarm. Toronto smells, he thought. There's no real air here, only smells. Hot greasy smells of hamburgers and French fries from a fast-food restaurant nearby; exhaust smells, the nose-prickling aromatic pinch of gasoline overlaid with sulphur, and the thick slow fumes of diesel trucks; wet garden smells from the girl in the long blue skirt selling roses for a dollar apiece; the smell of fresh newspapers from the stand at the corner; then all at once the wonderful smell of popcorn as a man pushing a whistling handcart stopped in front of him; the mingled smells of the lively nighttime crowd, perfume, beer, sweat, bodies sweet and sour; smells of smoke from uncountable pipes, cigars and cigarettes. Each smell was individual, distinct; each jostled the other in the cloud of odour that now Barney could almost swear was enveloping him. And over them all was a smell of hurry, of bustle, a smell of excitement.

Barney stood there unmoving. It wasn't that he was scared exactly. He just felt sort of numb; he felt all over the way his gums felt after the dentist had frozen them. Everything seemed to come to him through a filter, each sensation landing on him with a separate small thud, relentless, rapid, never stopping, so that he couldn't sort anything out. It was hard to think straight.

He shook himself a little, and his hand strayed to his pocket. He rubbed the top of Saki's head. "Okay, Sack," he whispered. "Let's go."

Dodging through the crowd, Barney moved towards the restaurant and ducked inside. There had to be a phone. Yep, over there, with a phone book five times thicker than the one in Chessborough. He flipped it open to the letter *O*. Oliver, Olson, Olthoff, Olympia Bowling — Olympia House. Barney's heart started to thump. He leaned against the booth, his knees abruptly weak.

There it was. It was real. Olympia House. Where his father lived. It was right there in black and white, in the telephone book. Gladness and relief spread through his throat in a rush. It was still there after ten years. It was a sign, he thought. It meant his father was still there too. He looked at the address, burned it into his memory.

"Hey, you gonna use the phone or not, kid?"

Barney jumped. He turned to see a waitress, shoulders drooped in fatigue, jingling some change in her uniform pocket.

"Uh, no. I was just looking up an address." He closed the directory and moved to go, then stopped. "Excuse me, but could you tell me where Gerrard is?"

"Gerrard Street? Yeah, it's about twelve blocks from here." The woman regarded him for a moment. "You new in town?" Barney nodded.

"Is it Gerrard East?" Barney nodded again. "Well, you go south at the corner" — she pointed — "till you're a couple of blocks past Carlton, then turn left on Gerrard. Okay?" She smiled. "Don't get lost now, ya hear?"

Barney smiled back at her. "Thanks a lot."

He headed south on Yonge and walked fast. Hayden, Charles, Isabella . . . As he counted off the blocks he began to feel better. That waitress had been okay. Friendly, even. Maybe people here weren't so bad. And the Olympia couldn't be too far away now . . . Wellesley Street . . . He saw a police cruiser at the corner, and two cops hustling a man into the back seat. His stride faltered for a moment; he moved closer to the buildings and walked a little faster.

Gerrard. He turned left.

None of the street names were familiar. Of course, he had been here only once before, when he was seven. It was in the summer, he remembered. He and his mom had gone on a magnificent spree to the C.N.E., the huge annual exhibition.

He smiled as he recalled how the Flyer had swooped and climbed, had hesitated so heart-stoppingly at the crest of each downward plunge, until the suspense inside him had built up so much he had wanted to shout in terror and delight. He and his mom had saved the Flyer for the last, and then they had gone on three times in a row.

That was some trip, he thought. Just his mom and himself. Without anybody else. They hadn't needed or wanted anybody else.

His smile disappeared. This trip sure wasn't like the first one. He looked around to get his bearings. Across the street, on a dimly lit sign hanging crookedly on a metal post, he could see the words: *Rooms by Day or Week. Olympia House.*

He ran towards it, then stopped. "What do you think, Saki?" he whispered to his companion. The mouse thrust his head inquisitively out of Barney's pocket, a moving patch of white against the dark denim. Barney was glad to have someone to talk to; his courage had deserted him, had evaporated into the summer night. He knew now that he had been fooled by the Olympia's grand-sounding name, fooled into expecting a hotel right out of the movies, where the windows shone, the pillars gleamed, and an army of clerks bustled about.

The Olympia House was not like that, not like that at all. It was old, worn-out, broken-down, a house that next month, next week, or perhaps even tomorrow would meet a quick and dusty death under the wrecker's ball. The entrance sported an ancient verandah, whose railing, minus a dozen uprights, looked like somebody with half his front teeth knocked out. Barney wondered how it had defied gravity for so long: it tilted and sagged, a monstrous architectural joke. The wrinkled skin of paint, spotted with soot, of no identifiable colour, had peeled here and there, only to reveal underneath a second layer as wrinkled, as spotted, as nondescript as the first.

To the east was a small park, a cramped square of green dotted with shrubs and trees. Several young couples strolled there, picking their way carefully to avoid the men with empty faces, old and not-so-old, who sat crumpled against the fence and sprawled on the wooden benches.

On the west side was a parking lot, and towards it the house leaned as if eavesdropping. Stuck on the outside wall, a set of firestairs, rustflecked and bent with time and weather, tumbled to a point three metres from the ground and then stopped abruptly.

Barney looked up. The place had three floors, the top floor squeezed by the diagonals of the roofline into only half a storey. The brick was old, crumbled at the corners, dingy with the accumulated grime of eighty years or more. The windows were like blind eyes, so soiled as to snuff out rather than reflect the light which rained upon them from the massive sign in the parking lot ten metres away. The pink neon message flickered and sizzled in the gathering darkness: *PARK PARK PARK 1.50 MAX ALL NITE*. Under it the landscape was changed into something strange and gaudy and carnival-like, and the house into a child's cartoon, crooked, rosy and improbable.

The front door was open. From the cracked ceiling hung a naked light bulb, its feeble rays serving only to deepen the shadows in the hall and on the staircase beyond. Barney felt a lump of disappointment settle into his stomach.

"Wow!" he whispered. Absently he stroked Saki, now perched on his left shoulder. "It sure doesn't look so hot, does it, Sack?" He hitched up his jeans and straightened his jacket. His breath left him in a sigh. "Well, here goes!"

Stepping around the broken concrete step and the hole in the porch floor, Barney lifted a horseshoe-shaped knocker, once fine brass, and let it drop twice against the chipped panel of the door. The sound echoed through the hall. No one came. Barney rapped again, three, four times.

Then he heard the slow rhythmic slap-slap-slap of slippers from somewhere in the back. He waited. Finally, around the curve in the hall, edging sideways around a rickety table, past a mirror fretted with black web-like lines where the silver had vanished, a woman shuffled towards him.

She was a remarkable sight. She was big, even fat, but it wasn't her size which made Barney stare — it was the colour. She was a walking rainbow! Above the pink fuzzy slippers which flopped on her feet she wore a bright yellow dress, with a wide purple belt encircling her middle. Enormous green earrings dangled beneath a mop of copper-coloured curls, while a heavy gold cross and a silvery four-leaf clover swung from her ample neck. On one arm bangles jingled as she walked; on the other hung a thick bracelet clustered with charms. Half a dozen gaudy rings flashed on her fingers.

As she reached the door and stood before him, Barney's eyes moved to her face. Her skin was fine and creamy, her eyes blue and alive and warm.

"Well, sonny?"

Barney stepped back a pace and at last found his voice. "Good evening, ma'am," he began. "I'm looking for Michael McGee."

The woman's eyes changed; her face closed over; what might have been a smile never materialized. "He ain't here." Her tone was clipped, discouraging. She started to shut the door. Barney lifted a hand to delay her, and as he did so a tawny striped shape slid from behind her. A split second later something furry flew through the air at Barney's face.

Saki dived into his neck and ran down his spine to lodge trembling at belt level. The cat, spitting and howling, clawed at Barney's shoulder where a moment earlier Saki had perched. Barney was too startled to move.

But the woman in front of him moved. Her arm flashed out and she seized the cat by the scruff of the neck, yanking it free.

"Tiger!" she shouted into its twitching ear. "Shame on you!" She shook the animal while it snarled and hissed like a dying sparkler. Then, with her arm straight out at shoulder height, she dropped it over the porch railing to the ground below. "Go raid the garbage!" she yelled as the cat disappeared across the parking lot.

Barney, bemused with surprise and the remnants of fright, rubbed the place where the cat had clung.

"I'm sorry, sonny. That cat ain't got no manners at all. He never done nothing like that before, though — I don't know what got into him." She peered at Barney and frowned.

"Well, ma'am," he said, still too surprised to lie, "he probably saw my mouse."

"You got a *mouse*, sonny?"

"Yeah, I do." He smiled. "Right now he's inside my shirt in the middle of my back, scared as anything."

To his amazement, the fat lady smiled back at him. Her low chuckle started like a distant freight train just gathering speed. Shuff. Shuff. Then it grew louder and faster and higher — chiff, chiff-chiff, chiff-chiff-chiff — until it climbed to a high soprano that made Barney shiver — heef-heef-heef-hee-hee-hee!

Barney stepped back and almost lost his balance. Suddenly he began to laugh with her.

When the storm had spent itself, the woman's face wore an expression of genuine concern. "Now, sonny, you better come in for a sec. That cat gave you a shock, I bet. You come on in and have a cup of tea. My name's Maggie, what's yours?"

Barney told her. He followed her down the hall and slid into a chair by a plastic-covered table in the kitchen. He watched as she dropped a teabag into an old mug with a picture of Niagara Falls on it and poured water from a battered steel kettle.

She placed the mug in front of him and smiled, her arms akimbo. "Now, Barney, why do you want to find Mickey McGee? How does a young fella like you even know the likes of him?"

Something in her voice made Barney uneasy. But he was too tired and too lonely to disguise his purpose any longer.

"He's my father."

Maggie's smile vanished. Her face was unreadable. Emotions flickered across it like the twitching illuminations of a strobe light, there and gone too fast to decode. She turned away from him as she asked, "Does Mickey know you're coming to visit?"

"No." Barney felt his face redden. "He — he left — he hasn't seen me in over ten years." Maggie said nothing. He rushed on. "And — and — it isn't just a visit. I'd kinda like to stay."

"Ummm." Maggie stood for a minute, gazing through the kitchen window, almost opaque with dirt, at the dim outlines of a scruffy tree in the tiny backyard. Then she turned decisively.

"Look, Barney, why don't you stay here and rest and have a bite to eat?" As she spoke she grabbed a jug of milk from the refrigerator and plucked a package of muffins from the counter near the sink. "Here, you just make yourself at home now. Maybe the mouse would like some cheese? It's in the fridge there, second shelf. You just set a while." She paused. "I think I can find your father for you. Don't worry."

* * *

I just gotta find him before it's too late, thought Maggie as she headed toward the benches on the far side of the little park adjoining the house.

Thank the Lord today was Sunday — Sunday he always went to the public bath down near the Salvation Army. At least he'd be clean.

By all the saints, what a mess! The poor kid back there coming from God knows where and God knows what kind of trouble to find his old man. Maggie shook her head in distress. To find Mickey McGee, who was hardly anybody's idea of a treasure. She quickened her step, glancing this way and that at the dozing men. Mike's favourite spot was over behind the clump of forsythia, out of sight of passersby. She picked her way around a pair of brawling dogs and a drinking fountain surrounded by barefoot kids before she spied him, sitting alone in the darkness. In two strides she was in front of him, reaching for the paper bag he had just lifted to his mouth.

"Gotcha, Michael McGee!" Her hand closed around the bottle hidden in the bag and snatched it away. "No more, Mickey."

"Aw, come on, Maggie, I've hardly had a drop the whole long day. Come on, now, give us the bottle, there's a lovely girl." His voice was tremulous, wheedling. He smiled up at the woman, and for an instant Maggie saw the young man, the winsome boy he must once have been. Like the one who now sat waiting in her kitchen.

"Mick, listen! You gotta straighten up! Your kid's here!"

The man's head snapped up. His faded eyes narrowed. "What do you know about my kid?"

80

"He's here, Mickey, he's here. He's over at the house right now."

"Oh, no." A groan escaped from the slack mouth. "Oh, no, Maggie! I don't want him to see me. That's over and done with long ago. That was another life. Tell him to go away, tell him I'm dead, tell him anything you like! Except the truth." Tears sprang to Mick's eyes and drifted down his veined cheeks.

Maggie shook him. "Mickey, stop it! You can do it. Just stay off the sauce for a couple of days and we'll figure out a way to send him home. Come on now! He came a long way. And he wants to see you awful bad."

The man grabbed her hand and held it tightly. "You think I can do it, Maggie?" She could feel the trembling clamminess of him. "If you help me, Maggie, maybe I can. I'll try. I'll try."

He got up, and still holding her hand, walked slowly towards the house. At first his steps were uncertain, shambling, like those of an old man, but as he reached the sidewalk they grew firmer.

His son. Mike tried to remember the boy's face, but could summon only a blur, only a recollection that he had once loved a little kid whose eyes and mouth were copies of his own. His son. His son had come to see him. At the door he pulled away from Maggie's supporting hand and straightened his frail body. His shoulders moved in a faint swagger. He smoothed back his hair, no longer thick or black, and forced his face into a grin. Then, with a cockiness borrowed from a past that seemed a hundred years ago, he strode into the kitchen like a buccaneer.

"Hi, Barney!"

Barney, drowsing at the table, his tea unfinished, came to with a start. His mind was fuzzy with fatigue. For a moment he peered timidly at the figure in front of him, shadowy in the dim light. Then he stood, smiled and moved to greet his father.

A day's work

The wind came up just before dawn. Blowing in from the east, it moved through the evergreen plantation north of Benedict like a giant's breath, forcing the piled clouds to flee before it, bending the tops of the trees, ruffling the feathery spruce branches till they seemed liquid. A small flock of grackles, awakening on their roost, felt their plumage stir and quicken as the breeze travelled past them; they unwrapped their iridescent wings, stretched and then, clacking with morning exuberance, launched themselves on the currents of air as if riding an invisible surf.

The river known as Peaceful Creek rippled as the wind blew across it. The reeds and rushes along the eastern bank swayed and drooped, obedient to the tempo of the air, and a denim hat, lodged at the base of a big cattail at the shoreline, escaped its indifferent prison. It snaked its way around the thicket of reeds and was caught by the current of deeper water. For a moment it rocked on the surface of the river, then spun on its brim and began to float downstream.

The sun rose, big and brassy in the clearing air, and sat on the rim of the earth like a cymbal waiting to clang. Long slanting rays filtered through the nets of spruce and poplar to pluck at the rippling river, making a lighted grid of its surface, a control panel with all the lights flashing. Little dots of brightness encircled the blue denim cap.

A sudden gust lifted the hat and sent it scudding towards the western bank. It moved into the shade of a jutting boulder and snagged momentarily on the rough surface. Bobbing, tacking, it freed itself and circumnavigated the stone, ambling closer to shore. Finally, in the twisted, finger-like roots of a dead oak, the hat was caught and held, brushing gently against the gravelly shore.

* * *

The sun had climbed halfway up the dazzling sky when Bill Conrad, following the OPP cruiser, turned the VW into Eddie's Service Station. He had been on the road for almost two hours, after a skimpy breakfast with Emily in the silent light of morning. Thinking now of her wan face, the bleakness in her eyes, he winced. Helplessness swept through him. He jammed on the brakes and jumped from the car.

"Now, Eddie," said Sergeant Vanderlinden, "let's have a look at that knapsack. Oh, this is Mr. Conrad, from Chessborough. Mr. Conrad, Eddie Rasminski."

Bill Conrad nodded an acknowledgement and followed Eddie into the office. He needed only one look. "It's Barney's."

Behind his glasses his eyes narrowed in pain. Through the long journey down he had hoped, against all reason, that a mistake had been made, that there would be some easy explanation to banish the dread. He had hoped all through the dawn, and all through the night before the dawn as he lay beside Emily, as sleepless as she, that Barney would appear, be found, return home.

Now even that dwarfed hope was gone. For a moment Conrad couldn't move. From some remote place he viewed the wreckage inside himself and was appalled; he felt torn in two. When he remembered how things had been between them before Barney left, remorse clawed at him, doubling his anguish. He drew a shaking breath.

"Have you searched the scene of the accident, sergeant?" he asked in a low voice.

"Got some men doing that now, sir."

"May I join them?"

Vanderlinden looked uncomfortable. His face clouded. He didn't much want a worried father getting in the way, but somehow he couldn't refuse.

"Well, I guess that would be all right, Mr. Conrad. Better come in my car." As he passed the candy counter Vanderlinden deftly picked an Oh Henry from the rack and stuck it in his pocket. "I owe you for a chocolate bar, Eddie," he called.

"I know how you must feel, Mr. Conrad," he said once they were in the car. "Got two kids of my own. But don't — don't jump to conclusions." Vanderlinden paused a moment before going on. "There are some funny things about this accident — we're not even sure your boy was in the car.

Seems likely, but — " The cruiser pulled out to pass a tractor.

"But what, sergeant?" Conrad's tone was urgent.

"Well, we can't figure out how the Moss kid got to shore. We're pretty sure, because of his injuries, that he was knocked out when he hit the water. But the passenger side was open." He paused again and shook his head. "It's still a puzzle. The boy could've been thrown out before the car reached the river. We'll know more once I talk to Harry Moss. I'll be going down to Toronto to interview him later on — the hospital says he's conscious now."

Hope rose in Bill Conrad. "You mean Barney could be around here somewhere?"

"Could be. We've got the area police alerted, and we'll start a search this afternoon."

Conrad was silent. Finally he said, "He was on his way to Toronto, sergeant. To — to find his — real father." The last words were little more than a whisper.

"Yeah. Chessborough filled me in, Mr. Conrad." Vanderlinden glanced at Conrad's face and said no more.

In another few minutes they pulled off the highway. Vanderlinden parked beside an open-doored van. As he alighted, Conrad could see oxygen tanks and ropes and ladders stacked neatly inside. Two constables in hip waders stood in the river a couple of metres from shore. Farther upstream a diver surfaced with a rippling splash, then submerged again. Conrad shivered and passed his hand over his eyes. My God! They were looking for Barney at the bottom of the river!

Vanderlinden walked down the gravelly bank to speak to his men. Bill Conrad followed slowly, then stopped. Somehow he couldn't bring himself to get too close. He walked downstream and crossed diagonally along a fisherman's footpath towards an old oak. He stood there for a few minutes in the morning sun. The river was well named, he thought idly. It was a beautiful spot. The sounds of the highway were muffled almost to silence; the quivering twang of insects, the rustle of full-leaved willows, the soft dark pulse of the water against the shore calmed him for a moment.

Then something caught his glance and he looked down at the roots of the dead tree. His heart began to beat too fast; his arms and legs tingled with it. He bent down and reached forward. Slowly his hand tightened on a blue denim cap.

* * *

Sure wish I hadn't lost my hat, thought Barney as he swung away from the hundredth mailbox of the morning. The canvas bag, stuffed with leaflets, smacked heavily against his right hip. The air shimmered with heat. Climbing now towards its highest point in the hazy city sky, the sun burned into his scalp, moistening his forehead and neck with perpetual sweat.

Mike had wakened him early. Before the sun was up they were standing in a back alley near

King and Sherbourne Streets, waiting for the door of a rundown office to open. A dozen others, men and boys, stood with them in the shadows. Some of the older men looked sick, Barney thought; their eyes and hands twitched as if controlled by a hidden motor, their clothes hung loose on their skinny bodies, their faces were blank and unshaven and grey.

Barney figured he was the youngest there. Closest to him in age was a boy about seventeen or eighteen slouching near the door, a real loudmouth who was arguing with a couple of the older men about last night's baseball game. Barney hoped they wouldn't get him as part of their delivery team.

But they did. When his father's name was called, when the groups of four had sorted themselves into the stripped-down Econoline vans, it was the loudmouth, the one they called Tippy (more like Lippy, Barney said sourly under his breath), who had squatted across from him in the dimness of the van's rear compartment. He had talked constantly, stopping only to spit between his feet and crack his gum.

And Tippy had been with them all morning. Barney could see him now, across the street in this quiet west Toronto suburb, slipping up to the houses and back. He was fast on his feet, smooth and skillful as he slid the advertising circulars under screen doors, swift at dodging, as Barney had not been, the barking rush of a jealous dog; he made the whole job seem a game, a graceful dancing game.

Barney shook his head wearily. If only he'd known last night what he knew now. His father had said he needed some money to show his son the town. Barney had offered the thirty-nine dollars left in his pocket but Mike had waved it away. "No, Barney," he had said. "I'm a little down on my luck right now, but I'm not about to take money from my only son." He had reached across the table in Maggie's kitchen and ruffled Barney's hair. "I tell you, boy, it's good to see you after all these years. I just wish you'd come sooner, before I lost my last job. It was a fine job, Barney, a good travelling job, on the road selling to the hotel trade. 'Course, that was a while back." His eyes had grown remote and his voice had dwindled to a whisper. "Yep, they were fine days, Barney, fine days — we would've had a grand time together, you and me."

Barney had laid a shy hand on his father's arm. "We still can, Mike."

Mike McGee had looked quickly at him, and then as quickly away. "Sure, Barney, sure we can," he had said, too loudly. "I'm certain to land another job soon, somethin' that fits my talents." He had turned his bright smile on Barney and clapped him on the shoulder. "Things'll work out. In the meantime I got a day's work lined up for tomorrow."

It was then, Barney remembered, that he had said, "I'll come with you!" Now, wiping the sweat off his neck, he found himself wishing he hadn't been quite so eager. The straps of the bag bit into his shoulder like thin wires. Funny — no matter how many leaflets he took out, the bag never got any lighter. He caught up to his father three houses ahead — they'd been working the same side of the street. Tippy had finished his side and was lounging on the curb waiting for them.

"Hurry up, Mike," yelled Tippy. "Truck'll be here in five minutes. You're really slowin' down lately, old man." The youth's eyes narrowed and grew sly. He reached into the bottom of his bag and pulled out a bottle of whiskey. "Need a little pick-me-up, Mike?" Tippy laughed, his mouth curving meanly. He unscrewed the cap of the bottle and took a long swallow. Then he held it out to Barney. "Want a drink, kid?"

"Lay off, Tippy," Mike said.

"What's the matter, old man? Don't you want the kid to follow in your footsteps?"

Barney saw his father's face turn ashen, his lips tighten into a thin line as he lunged toward the lolling youth. Tippy laughed and rolled out of the way. "Take it easy, Mike. Here, no hard feelings. Have a swig."

Mike's face twitched and his hand stretched out as if pulled by invisible strings. Barney stared at him, confused and dimly frightened. Mike met the stare for an instant and his hand dropped. Sweat sprang from his forehead and ran down his cheeks.

"No thanks, Tippy. You need it more than I do, for sure!"

Tippy's eyes changed into slits again and a flush darkened his pimply skin. "You take the pledge, McGee? Or are you just showin' off for your kid?"

"I'm warnin' you, Tippy, keep your mouth shut," snarled Mike.

"What's wrong, Mike, you scared to take a drink? Hey? You chicken?"

Barney watched as his father's face twisted in anger and misery and a kind of helplessness. Suddenly, with an explosive curse, Mike moved forward and grabbed the bottle from Tippy. He sucked at it noisily once, twice, three times, then thrust it away from him with a shaky hand.

"No, you son of a — " he said in a trembling hiss to the smiling Tippy. "I ain't scared."

The van swung around the corner and braked to a stop beside them.

The moment of truth

The afternoon was like the morning. Only hotter. And longer. The suburb was different but the houses, the doors, the dogs, the letterboxes all seemed the same. Barney's feet protested every step. His elbow hurt. The sun beat down like a blacksmith's hammer.

Even Saki, tucked in the pocket of Barney's unbuttoned shirt, was hot. His breath was a rapid flutter against the skin of Barney's chest. He had cooled off once or twice in birdbaths along the route, but Barney knew the mouse was as unhappy as he was. When would this terrible job be done?

Barney moved like an automaton up a walk, folding a circular as he went, slipping it into the letterslot or under the door without losing stride, down the walk, reaching into the canvas bag for yet another of the never-ending supply. Without conscious command, his hands moved and his feet moved, parts of the delivery machine he had now become. He felt as if he'd been doing this all his life.

He glanced at his watch. Only another hour and the van would pick them up. He reached the end of the street and looked around. No sign of Mike. No sign of Tippy. The street was empty. He shaded his eyes against the sun and peered both ways — no sign of anybody.

Crossing the street, Barney walked ahead to a back alley leading north. He turned into it and scanned its length. Twenty metres away he saw his father and Tippy leaning against a garbage can. They were laughing and passing a bottle back and forth.

Barney watched for a moment, his stomach tightening with a sensation that was new to him, yet not new. It was something he seemed to remember from a long time ago, something his nerves remembered on their own, a reflex of fear that had lain in wait for years and years to ambush him now. He felt a little sick.

Then he saw Tippy and Mike pull what was left of the leaflets from their dirty canvas carriers. Laughing, the two of them stuffed the papers into the garbage can.

Barney walked slowly towards them. His father looked up. His mouth hung loose in an empty grin. "C'mon, Barn, las' stop! Get ridda those damn things right in here! Best damn mailbox in town!" He giggled.

Sweat dripped from Barney's armpits; it crawled like a troop of worms across his forehead and around his ears. His skin throbbed with heat. But inside of him he felt as if a chunk of ice had settled, blocking his lungs.

His father was drunk. And Barney knew it wasn't the first time. He pushed the thought away and ran to the two men.

"Mike! Hey, come on! You can't do that!" Barney reached into the garbage can and pulled out the sheaf of circulars. Nervously he smoothed them out, his fingers plucking at their curled edges. "What're you doing, anyway?" His voice cracked and for a moment he heard himself sound like a little boy. He cleared his throat.

"What are you doing, Mike?" he asked again. He looked at his father's face, then looked away. He could feel Tippy's eyes on him and swung to meet his glance. Tippy was staring at him curiously, as if wondering why he was so upset. Barney's teeth gritted as he said, "I can see you're a real pal of my father's!"

"Why, sure thing, Barney! I always try to give the old man what he wants!"

Barney turned away, anger and nausea fighting in his chest. A crazy mixture of feelings overcame him, leaving him without speech — fright and shame and an odd sense of betrayal, a feeling of losing something he had clung to for years, something that had now vanished into the rotten sweaty air of this rotten August afternoon in rotten Toronto. Then suddenly, slicing through it all like a cool breeze, came a quick vision of the woods outside Chessborough where Timberline Creek ran down to the lake in little rushing bubbles.

He turned back to his father. "I'll finish these papers, Mike, and then we'll get home. The van'll be here in half an hour. Can you make it to the pickup point?"

"Sure," Mike mumbled.

Tippy's glance slid away from Barney's. He put an arm around Mike's skinny shoulders. In a low voice he said, "I'll see he gets there, Barney."

Barney walked away, his steps stiff and slow, his fingers seeking and stroking Saki's velvety head.

* * *

Nell fidgeted in the vinyl-covered chair, then rose with the rest as Judge Legrand entered the courtroom. The case was one of hers, a child of eleven who was an accomplished shoplifter. The parents sat two rows forward, their backs rigid and uncompromising. Their daughter sat between them. It had been they, Nell remembered, who had insisted the girl be brought to court, claiming she was wicked and needed to be punished. Nell was sure they had already punished her. She had seen the child at the hospital a month ago, with her back and legs covered with bruises, bruises her father had insisted she got from falling downstairs.

Nell shook her head. After one gentle conversation with the girl she had diagnosed the problem. The poor kid wanted affection so badly, affection her parents withheld, that she had decided to get it from her admiring classmates by stealing whatever they wanted from downtown department stores. The story was clear enough, and distressingly common. Nell had already drafted a report to the judge.

It was hot in the courtroom. Air conditioning on the fritz again, Nell thought. Third time this summer. A young law clerk, dapper, self-important, began to recite the particulars of the case. His pompous monotone drifted through the muggy air, each syllable landing on Nell's ears like a wet mitten.

She glanced toward the bench and smiled. Even Judge Legrand, who usually looked as if he'd been freshly starched, seemed wilted. The folds of his robe had abandoned their perfect parallel corrugations and fallen into rumples. The white upright collar, most of the time as stiff and unbending as its owner, had curled its corners in protest. And twice now the judge had removed his gold-rimmed glasses and patted his enormous forehead with a handkerchief so sternly white it dazzled. She guessed he would probably remand today.

Her mind wandered a little. Absently she scratched the back of her neck where yesterday a mosquito had found a juicy target. Wonder where Barney is, she mused. She hadn't been able to put him out of her mind. All night long, in her restless and dream-dogged sleep, the boy's eyes, big and dark in the bright face, had appeared and reappeared. Every now and then Saki's whiskered triangular features would pop up beside the boy's, and a hawk would scream. Wonder how they are, she thought. Wonder if he'll ever call me.

Judge Legrand's gavel crackled like a pistol shot. Nell jumped.

"Remanded thirty days in parents' custody. Mrs. Weatherston to prepare pre-sentence report."

The black robe swished as Judge Legrand rose and exited.

Nell smiled encouragingly at the pinched face of the little girl, and sighing with heat and something she could not name, left the Family Court building.

* * *

In the huge old hospital a few blocks west, on the second floor, a young man lay on an unbending mattress and stared at the ceiling, wondering how to escape. The fuzz from Benedict had left a few minutes ago. Harry had trouble remembering what the cop had asked him. Or what he had answered. Not that it mattered. He just knew he had to get away. The place was likely crawling with cops, but he was sure he could give them the slip. He knew the caper. If only his head would stop hurting . . .

Everything was so mixed up. He remembered picking up the kid who said his name was Johnny. But that wasn't his name; the cop had called him Barney something-or-other. And he remembered asking the kid for his money. But after that it was all a blank. Bits of recollection, sudden feelings, sensations, blurred images of dark sky and rushing water bobbed briefly to the surface of his memory and then sank like stones to some unreachable place.

The sergeant said they had found him on the shore. How did he get to shore if he had been out cold in the river? He must have swum. Harry frowned in frustration. His brain felt adrift in fog. Everything was at a distance except the pain grinding at the front of his skull, now bearing a thick bandage. Bad concussion, they said. Lucky to be alive, they said. Unconscious for two days, they said. Then how the hell did he get to shore?

A wisp of something, a phantom or a dream, stirred and rose in Harry's clouded memory. He remembered a motion, a shadowy sense of being pulled or dragged or moved somehow from one place to another. He lay still, his face creased in concentration. He forced his mind to relax, to wait for that one piece to the puzzle, the key to the mystery. He knew what had happened. If only he could focus on it . . . A moment passed, immeasurable, then another. All at once his mind leaped in a split-second surge of clarity and flashed a picture.

Harry let out his breath. He was soaked in sweat. But he knew. He knew what had happened in the river. The boy had saved him. Barney, the kid he was going to rob, the kid he had slashed with the knife, had pulled him from the car and dragged his body to shore.

Harry shut his eyes. His head hurt worse. Why had the kid done that? He couldn't figure it out. Why hadn't the kid just left him to drown? Why did he want to save a guy who had just carved him up? Harry couldn't understand it. In his whole life nobody had ever done him any favours. And he had never asked for any.

Harry struggled to open his eyes, to escape the soft feathery dark waiting to surround him. There was something he should do, something . . . He pushed himself up on his elbows and pressed the call button. A nurse materialized at his door.

"Ma'am, will you get a message to that cop who was here? Tell him the kid is probably okay. He's the one who got me out of the river. Tell the cop I remember what happened."

He fell back, spent, and tried once again to marshal his thoughts. He had to get out of here . . .

* * *

Two hundred kilometres away a lean and bony man, shoulders slumped from their customary right angles, stared out at the orange afternoon sun. His hands rested, idle, on the blue and white teapot he had just repaired. Emily Conrad came to the kitchen door, then with a swift step crossed the room to touch her husband's drawn face.

Bitter memories

Barney grabbed his father's arm and pulled him back into the lane. Ten metres away, in front of the Olympia House, a yellow police cruiser sat like a huge humming wasp.

"Stay back, Mike! There's a cop car in front of Maggie's. They're probably looking for me."

Mike stared blearily at him, not understanding. He leaned against the soot-scarred brick of the old building, grateful for the rest, willing to stay there in the coolness of the narrow alley for as long as his son demanded. He was thirsty. He hoped dimly that Tippy would remember his promise to leave two bottles of sherry under the back porch. "Can't trust the young punk, though," he mumbled under his breath. "Like as not drink it himself." His tongue ran around the dry crevices of his mouth. Lord, he needed a drink! If he could just have a few to straighten himself out, just a few. Then he and Barney could maybe have a nice talk tonight, get to know one another, make some plans. If he could just have a few drinks, not too many, not so he'd mess up and disappoint the kid, just a few . . . Mike sighed with heat and weary thirst.

Barney looked around the corner of the building. Two shirt-sleeved constables, holster straps bisecting their chests, walked with measured steps to the cruiser. As they reached the sidewalk one of them turned and yelled, "Don't forget now, Maggie. If a kid comes around asking for McGee, we want to know!"

"Sure thing, officer, sure thing," Maggie shouted back. "You bet! First sign I see of this kid I'll get right on the phone. Don't worry. This ain't no place for a kid anyway."

The policeman grunted and climbed into the car beside his companion. The vehicle moved slowly east along Gerrard and turned south at the first intersection.

Barney grinned. He beckoned to Mike. "It's okay. Come on!" Good old Maggie. She had covered for him beautifully. She was one great lady. In more ways than one, he reflected, smiling. Funny, though, how he no longer thought of her as odd or fat. He saw her now simply as good old Maggie.

She stood on the grey sloping porch, arms folded across her chest, watching father and son approach up the cracked cement walk. As Mike drew nearer, her plump features, satiny with heat, clouded over. She peered at him closely, sniffed as he reached the top step. She glanced at Barney.

He met her eyes. A message was sent and received, a message that needed no words to make it clear. As Barney stepped around her, she dropped a warm hand on his shoulder and murmured, "He'll be all right, Barney. I'll make some coffee and bring it upstairs."

Barney felt his body slump into fatigue as he climbed the grimy stairs behind his father, the same stairs which only yesterday had seemed to be a pathway to hope and adventure and a different, wonderful life. He clutched the banisters for support, used them as a mountain-climber might a rope. Two steps above him, his father tripped. Barney steadied him, noting how wrinkled and shabby Mike's shirt and pants looked in the light from the casement window on the landing. Four more stairs. Two. There.

Barney half stumbled into the room and sat down heavily in the sagging armchair by the window. He had never in his life been so tired. He was too tired to think, too tired to do anything but sit. His hand reached toward his shirt pocket. He lifted Saki free and placed him on the arm of the chair, where the stuffing spilled out in a grey ropy mass. Digging a handful of sunflower seeds from his jeans, he spread them in front of the mouse. Watching the little creature, Barney was abruptly overcome by a feeling that Saki was his only friend, the only remaining link to a world Barney had once — long ago, it seemed now — been able to understand.

He kept his eyes carefully away from his father. He could hear Mike at the other side of the room, hear him breathing, hear him mutter to himself every now and then. Twice he caught the name "Tippy."

The door bounced open and Maggie entered, balancing a tray on one upheld hand. She looked as if she'd done it before. On the tray were sandwiches and three big mugs of coffee, steam swirling lazily around their rims, leaving a thin moisture.

"Here we are, men!" Her voice was cheerful, almost gay, as she swung her burden down to the spotted, cigarette-burned card table. "Time to eat!" Her eyes slid from the boy to the man in a nervous flutter.

Barney smiled up at her, glad of her solid presence. He looked at the food and was suddenly ravenous. Mike mumbled something about the bathroom and shuffled from the room. Barney could feel the tension in Maggie as she turned to watch him go. He stirred in the chair, shrugged off his uneasiness. Swiftly he picked up an enormous ham and cheese on rye, the meat curling out between the bread slices in thick pink petals, the Swiss cheese chunky and fresh. He took as big a bite as his mouth could manage.

Barney started to feel better. Maybe things would work out. Maybe he could stay. Maybe Mike would . . . The sentence hung in his mind, incomplete. Somehow he couldn't finish it, didn't know how to finish it.

He took another bite.

* * *

Mike had hardly touched the food, in spite of Maggie's anxious urging. He had left the room a couple of times, once to get some air, another time to find ice cubes. He said his coffee was too hot. He seemed livelier now, Barney thought. He was laughing, talking, almost the way Barney had dreamed he would be when he had first gazed at the hidden snapshot in his mother's bedroom.

Saki danced on the card table, preparing to feast on the few crusts and crumbs left from the trayful of sandwiches. Barney smiled, remembering how Maggie had eaten Mike's share and more, claiming all the while that she wasn't really hungry, it was only that she didn't like to waste food. She had just now gone downstairs, swearing under her breath at the distantly ringing telephone.

The room was peaceful, hushed. The last rays of the sun seeped through the window, casting a faint greenish light over the walls, the bed, the chair, his father's face. Barney had a fleeting sense of being underwater, or in the middle of a jungle. Everything seemed slowed down, blurred around the edges, resting.

"That's a nice mouse, Barney. Real smart." Barney looked sharply at his father. "Mouse" had sounded like "moush."

"Yeah," he answered, noncommittal, careful.

"I r'member I had a pet too when I was a kid. A rabbit." Mike smiled and his face was like that of a child. "Sure was a nice rabbit. White, he was. With brown ears. Called him Brownie." He smiled again.

Barney smiled too. All at once he warmed to Mike, feeling easy in the velvet gloom, relaxed and happy for the first time since he had left Chessborough. This was part of what he had hoped for, what he had run away to, this quiet evening time with his real father. He leaned forward. The springs of the old chair complained in a grinding squeal. "What happened to him, Mike?"

"What happened to what?" Mike looked confused, his eyes blank.

Barney was disconcerted. "The — the rabbit — Brownie," he stammered. He squinted again at his father.

"Oh. Yeah." Mike got up from the battered chrome chair. "Just a minute, son. I'll tell ya all about it. Just gotta go down the hall for a sec."

Barney frowned, puzzled. He looked around the room as if he were seeing it for the first time. He shivered slightly, despite the muggy heat trapped from the day. The tattered green linen blind reached halfway down the window, its edges ravelled, the sizing gone long ago, each tiny tear and crack in its ancient surface filling up with twilight. It flapped once or twice in the breeze, which rose from the lane below like a lazy thief. It was still hot. The pavement of the busy street sent out invisible waves of warmth. Sweat dampened Barney's forehead and neck. But again he shivered.

Saki finished the crusts. Sitting back, he moistened his pink forepaws and rubbed his whiskers with a banker's seriousness. Then he reached behind the translucent triangles of his ears to remove imaginary dirt. Barney watched abstractedly for a moment, then jumped out of the armchair. The smouldering butt of his father's cigarette had rolled off the old tin ashtray, and it now lay almost touching Saki's tail. Barney picked it up and crushed it out.

"Here we are, kid. Brought us a Coke." Mike swayed in the doorway, two bottles of pop in his hands. One was half empty. He passed the full bottle to the boy. "This one's for you, Barn, old son." He smiled loosely, ingratiatingly, as if the Coke were a peace offering. "And," he muttered, moving towards the rumpled bed, "this one here is for Mickey." He settled on the bed, his head propped against the wall, and let out a long sigh.

"Now what was it we were talkin' about, lad?"

Barney couldn't answer. His tongue felt locked in behind the bars of his teeth. Besides, what could he say? There was no point in talking. No point in pretending any more. The truth was there in front of him.

"Oh, yeah, the rabbit," said Mike. His eyes misted with memory. "I loved him, y'know. Yep, I sure loved that rabbit." He coughed, and drank once more from the pop bottle. "I got him for Easter the year I was seven. From my old gran. He was white. With brown ears. Did I tell you that, Barn? I named him Brownie." Mike heaved himself upright for a moment and leaned forward, his eyes shining. "Y'know, Barn, I actually taught him to do some tricks! He could sit up and beg, just like a dog! He sure was a smart rabbit."

Suddenly Mike's face clouded over and he fell back against the pillow. His head hit the wall with a muffled thud.

106

Barney's voice was a creaky whisper when it finally emerged. He looked everywhere but at his father. Knowing he was only making conversation, he asked without expression, "How long did you have him, Mike?"

There was no answer. A minute passed, then another. Barney listened to his own breathing. Finally he looked up. Tears were streaming down his father's flushed cheeks, and thin sobs made his body arch and jump as if an electric shock were coursing through it.

Alarmed into speech, Barney cried, "Mike! What's wrong?"

"Ah, Barney, it was a cruel thing to do, a cruel thing!" Mike's sobs grew louder. Tears splashed on his chin and dropped to his chest.

Barney stepped to the bed and took his father's hand. *What* was a cruel thing, Mike? Tell me, please!"

Mike hiccupped. He took a long swallow from the bottle, and liquid dribbled from the corners of his mouth and crept down the creases of his chin like blood. Barney watched, fascinated. Almost like having veins on the outside, he thought crazily.

His father spoke again in a trembling rasp. "I had a little hutch for him out in the backyard. And one day I forgot to lock it. I was in a hurry to go swimmin' with the other kids. It was in August and hot, and I didn't close the hutch tight. Like he was always yellin' at me to do. I was near halfway to the river 'fore I remembered. And then I ran like hell all the way home."

He hiccupped again. Two more tears drifted downwards. "But I was too late. I was too late, Barney! Brownie was out in the garden chewin' the buds off my dad's stupid flowers. He loved those damn flowers, Barney, more'n anything — more'n his wife, and for sure more'n his kid. I was just through the gate when he came runnin' out the back door, screamin' like a lunatic, with a shotgun in his hands. I yelled at him to stop, but he didn't hear me. And he wouldn't 've listened anyhow. Brownie was sittin' there havin' a fine old time one minute and the next minute his head was blown off."

Mike started to cry again. Barney held his hand tighter, not knowing what to say, aware only of a deep pain in his chest. "Ever hear a rabbit scream, Barn? It's an awful sound. Brownie screamed. Just the once. And then I screamed, I guess. I don't remember." His face darkened and went hard. "But I still remember my stinkin' rotten father shootin' Brownie to pieces."

Mike shuddered, tilted the bottle up and emptied it. Barney could look at him now. The room was dusky with moonlight; their voices were softer, muted, as the dark enveloped them. His anger and his fear had drained away. All he felt was grief for the seven-year-old Mickey McGee who had lost his rabbit.

Worn out, Barney lay down beside his father. Mike smiled a little, made room for him, lit a cigarette. The tip glowed and faded, faded and glowed in an intermittent signal before Barney's drooping eyes. As he drifted into sleep he heard the faint rumble of Mike's snore beside him.

* * *

Saki's nose twitched. He lay in an empty tobacco tin on a little mat of shredded paper. He moved his head from side to side, up and down. His nose twitched again. Drifting through the top of the tin came the smell of something that made the fine hairs of his coat rise in wary fright, something that rang an alarm in his muscles and whiskers, a choking thick warm something that smelled of danger and death. He burrowed deep into his nest.

Sirens in the night

Ten blocks west, its four sides a bright pattern of windows, the hospital thrust its huge bulk into the sky. Inside, the building rustled with the routine of a shift change. It was eleven o'clock.

Bev Wilton, the head nurse of the night staff, sat down behind the partition at the second floor station and put on her glasses. With a sigh she began to scrutinize the charts. Axler, Curtis, Dimitri, Finster . . . Everything okay. She yawned a little and disguised it with one hand. First night back after three weeks on days. Always took some getting used to. She shook her head to clear it. Lennie, McCarthy, Moss — room 206. The name didn't register for a moment. Oh, yes, he was the kid from up north, admitted on her day off. He had been asleep, she remembered, when she had made rounds a few minutes earlier.

Quickly she scanned his chart. "Head wound, concussion — check frequently," read the special instructions. And in red capitals across the top of the page, *SECURITY*. Bev nodded to herself, remembering the young police officer in front of the boy's room. But with that diagnosis there shouldn't be any trouble. He'd be in and out of sleep most of the time. And, she mused, he didn't look old enough to have done much wrong. She flipped a few pages to the social history. Nell

Weatherston's case. She read the three terse paragraphs synopsizing the life of seventeen-year-old Harold Moss and her lips thinned. Poor kid. Maybe Nell could help him. If anybody could. Peterson, Renwick, Stavroff, Thompson . . . Bev yawned again.

Five doors down the hall to the left, Constable Chisholm stood up and stretched, pulling his starched blue shirt half out of the heavy regulation trousers. Another hour before his relief came. He was bored. He'd sooner be out on the beat. Or even directing traffic. Could use some coffee, he thought, glancing down the hall at the vending machine near the desk. He felt in his pocket for some change. He started to move away from room 206, then halted in midstride and retraced his steps. Noiselessly turning the handle, he opened the door a crack and peered inside. Eyes closed, face pale and bluish in the reflected fluorescence of the city lights, the boy lay still, his regular breathing marked by the gentle rise and fall of the bedspread. Out cold again, thought Chisholm as he closed the door. He walked down the hall, his cleated boots making a dull, metallic rhythm on the tiles.

Harry opened his eyes. It was now or never. Throwing off the spread, he sat up and swung out of bed. He was clad in the jeans and denim shirt, found in the bedside commode, which he had put on — was it four days ago? — back at his uncles' farm.

His mouth twisted. He wouldn't see that place again, he promised himself in a whisper.

111

He'd never go back. He'd keep on moving till he found a place where nobody would hassle him. His whole life had been nothing but a hassle. The only decent thing that had ever happened to him was that kid pulling him out of the river. He still couldn't figure that one out.

Swiftly he bunched the covers and spare pillow together to make an inert copy of his own sleeping body. Then, grabbing his running shoes, he made his way without a sound toward the dim oblong of window which looked down on the wide sweeping entrance to Emergency one floor below. Hurrying now, he jammed his feet into the worn runners and tied the laces into double knots. What he had to do in the next few minutes needed sure and nimble steps.

The window was old, framed in wood. Flaking layers of green paint had faded to the colour of parsnips. Harry reached up to the lock in the middle rail and pressed the metal lip towards the pane. It moved only a fraction, sealed in place by decades of paint. Sweat sprang out on his forehead as he reached again, pressed again. It moved another millimetre. He whispered a curse, and stepping back a pace, pressed once more, leaning his full weight against it. It moved again, and then unlocked with a soft snap.

Harry pressed his hot face against the cool glass for a moment, holding his breath against the pain of his cracked ribs. His heart was beating faster than it should and his knees felt weak. He looked out the window again to verify what he had discovered that morning: to the right, about six metres from him, the brick wall jutted out at right angles, and on its face was a large window, propped open with a piece of wood. Probably put there by a janitor trying to get some air, Harry thought. The window was just above the canopy which sheltered the ambulances driving into Emergency. Through its dulled glass Harry could see the subdued scarlet glow of an exit light. If he could just get to that window . . .

With both hands he shoved sharply upward; to his surprise, the bottom pane moved easily. He leaned out and looked along the wall. There was a ledge — not much of a ledge but still a ledge — which ran across the brick wall from window to window, as far as he could see. About a metre to his right was another window, companion to the one he had just opened. Its sill formed a concrete chin in line with the fancy ledge. There lay his sidewalk to freedom.

He ducked his head back in and listened. Beyond the door someone murmured something, and a chair leg scraped against the floor. The fuzz was back. Harry took a deep, sighing breath, and bending his weakened muscles, pulled himself up and through the window to stand on the sill outside. He looked down — then looked up again fast. The ground, a dark sweep of curved asphalt, looked hard and unyielding. Slowly he turned his body to face the building; slowly he moved along the ledge, his ribbed running shoes gripping the weathered cement. Taut with purpose, his hands seeking the broken channels of mortar between the bricks, he crept across the shadowy face of

113

the building as a stalking lizard might creep over the desert sand. He reached the neighbouring window and went on. At the corner he paused. His muscles, stretched with tension, felt like lead weights in his limbs. His head continued to ache, a dull throb spurting outward from his forehead in remorseless ripples of pain, like a stone thrown into a pond. He blinked again and again, bending his face to his shirt-sleeve to blot the endless sweat.

With fingertips that felt like someone else's, he clung to the powdery crevices. He peered into the dimness in front of him to find the ledge on the angled wall, to find a place for his searching foot. At that moment a taxi swerved into the driveway and for a second its headlights lit the window which was his goal. He flattened himself against the brick. The corner would be tricky. The ledge stopped, then began again on the other wall some distance lower, and in from the corner. For the space of a footstep there would be nothing to stand on but air.

Harry forced himself not to look down, focusing only on the wall in front of him. He stepped out and across and down, his hands gripping desperately. His left foot found the ledge and he leaned for a moment against the wall, striving for a new balance. His right foot dangled in space, found a corner to rest on, then suddenly slipped. Panic raced through Harry's blood like fire as his knee hit the ledge. He clung, whimpering like an animal, the sweat pouring from his body. Painfully, slowly, he dragged himself up, every muscle trembling with effort and fear, until he had both feet on the ledge next to the window. The gauze bandage around his head was soaked. He hoped it was only sweat.

Carefully he slid to the security of the sill, his arm hooking around the window's edge. There! Another step and he stood framed in the big window, a black crucifix against the pink glow of the exit sign inside. Relief and a weary triumph engulfed him.

Just then a mournful duet of sirens broke out as an ambulance and a cruiser, lights flashing, screamed around the corner half a block away, their terrible alarms climbing in a lonely crescendo before dropping to a moan as they turned, tires squealing, up the drive to Emergency. Headlights and flashers played for an instant like darting luminous fish over Harry's spread-eagled body.

Cops! The thought made his blood freeze. Without thinking, he pushed his legs through the open window, wriggled the rest of his body after them, and landed on the marble floor of the stairwell. He huddled there, his heart pounding with fatigue and fright, his breath coming in rasps.

He smiled. He had made it. The rest would be a snap. He would get away, lose himself in the huge city and start fresh. Down three stairs to his right was the grey shape of a door. Harry straightened up and moved towards it.

* * *

In the dream, Barney struggled. In the dream, an enormous hand pressed on his chest. No matter which way he turned, as he wrenched himself from left to right, from right to left, the hand squeezed and squeezed, tighter and tighter, wrapping fingers thick as truck tires around his chest and throat.

He tried to sit up but he couldn't move. And without moving, somehow he fell even deeper into a black pit. He opened his mouth to scream and suddenly found himself coughing and choking, wide awake to the terror not of his dream but of the nightmare reality around him. The room was solid with smoke, a smothering sea of dense shadow which he could almost gather in his flailing arms. He tried again to shout, but a spasm of choking closed his throat. His nose felt seared, his eyes were blind, helpless, streaming with water. He turned over and pounded on his father's skinny back. "Mike!" he rasped. "Mike!"

His father mumbled something and coughed.

"Mike! We gotta get out! Fire!" Barney's words were gasps. His father didn't move. Frantic, Barney scrambled over Mike's body and clutched his hands. He pulled. "Mike! Come on!"

His father fell out of bed to the floor. The thump and the clearer air roused him. He sat up coughing. "That way, Barn!" he choked out. "To the fire escape!"

They crawled along the splintery floor, past the flames which Barney could now see burning like signals of distress around the edges of the tattered rug and along the scuffed baseboard, reaching hungrily for the ravelled plastic table cloth, the sagging slipcover on the big wing chair, the old newspapers in a pile by the flimsy hotplate, the paint on the scarred table. The noise was like a thousand dry branches stepped on at once, all around them, closing in.

Abruptly Barney bumped into his father's legs and felt a quick rush of air on his face. "This way! Through the door!" Mike's voice was a harsh blur swallowed by the hiss of the fire.

The hall was an acrid, swirling murk. Below them, on the lower floors, Barney heard shouts, excited cries of "Fire!" as the other roomers scurried from their beds; footsteps, muffled by the billowing blackness, hurtled down remote stairs; car horns blared distantly; and somewhere, blocks away, through the humid city air a fire siren howled.

In another agonized minute they were outside on the rickety metal platform of the fire escape. Barney stretched out beside his father; they lay panting, lungs battling to capture the sweet air, faces streaked like a zebra's hide with sweat and soot. Mike finally struggled to his knees.

"Okay, Barn, you go first. Down the ladder. I'll be right behind you."

Barney moved to obey. Then he stopped short and moaned. "Saki! We forgot Saki!" He turned to go back.

Just then a ceiling-high wave of smoke swelled out of the room they had left. Flames lapped at the paint of the door frame, which blistered and peeled and became what consumed it. The wallpaper beside it, loose on the decaying plaster, flared brightly, a bone-coloured gash in the dark. The heat rushed at them as if a huge furnace had suddenly swung open.

"You can't go back!" yelled Mike, and his pale scrawny arms, with an unsuspected strength, held the boy fast. "Go! Down the ladder!" He lifted the boy and carried him to the edge of the platform, then kicked savagely at the ladder to loosen it from its rusty mooring. It didn't budge. He kicked again, in vain. Below him, through the smoke, he saw a blood-red ladder truck flickering in the glare as if it too were ablaze, and a fireman steadily climbing towards them. Barney was crying, screaming, his fists pounding at his father's arms and chest. "Let go, Mike! Let me go! I gotta get Saki!"

Mike heard his son's scream echo in the night, heard an earlier scream, silent and deep, somewhere inside himself. He shoved Barney at the fireman and turned away. He stood for a moment in the doorway, his shirt the only whiteness in the dreadful black. Then he disappeared.

A cry wrenched itself from Barney's throat, and a great sigh went up from the crowd of watchers. Then, except for the angry choir of the flames, there was a strange hush, a sense of waiting. And suddenly, above the upturned, expectant faces, a figure lurched to the metal railing, hair aflame like a halo, clothes charred to ashy tatters. An "oh" of shock and pity rose from the crowd. The figure cried out in a voice not quite human, "Barn, I saved him! I saved him!"

118

Mike held the tobacco tin aloft in a blackened fist before dropping it to Barney's waiting hands.

Sick with dread, the boy lifted out the body of the little mouse. It was limp; the eyes were closed. "Saki! Saki!" Barney cried. Then he heard a faint indignant squeaking as one bright eye opened and looked up. The rush of tears made him blind, but not before he saw the figure on the fire escape, arms outstretched, sway forward against the rusty rail and slowly, like a sack of coal, topple to the ground below.

Barney's choice

Nell Weatherston raked a weary hand through her grey curls and wondered again, wryly, why she was sitting here. Sitting here in the hospital cafeteria drinking yet another cup of coffee at — she glanced up at the big digital clock and translated the 2300 hours and some minutes into something her old-fashioned arithmetic could grasp — eleven-fifteen at night.

Because she didn't have sense enough to go home, she supposed. Because home wasn't really home at all, just an empty apartment three blocks away that she couldn't bear tonight, whose walls were anonymous, whose rooms held no memories.

Absently she stirred her coffee again. Home was really right here in this hospital where every hall, every ward, every corner had known her footstep these last thirty years, where she had shared so many of the lives — and eased a few of the deaths — of her young charges, shared their joys and griefs and hopes.

And the children here — especially since that day last December — had been all she had of family. Some had claimed her more than others: seven-year-old Debbie who couldn't walk, happy now in the home Nell had found for her, happy with the parents and brothers in that home; Joey, once — until he was jumped by somebody meaner and tougher — the meanest, toughest streetkid in the city, now a gentle music student at the Conservatory; white-faced, unsmiling Angela in the courtroom today; and that new boy on Station Two — what was his name? Harry — Harry Moss, that was it.

Now that one had problems, she reflected, remembering the history, the comments of the police, the youth's own curled-lip hostility. And yet there had been something there, something soft and vulnerable in his look when she had talked with him earlier, much too briefly, before he drifted away into the drowsiness which had held him ever since his admission. There had been something in his eyes that had pleaded for help, that had called to a part of her she had believed long buried in scars.

Why, she asked herself again, was she sitting here? Why was she fretting over some teenage hood from a small town up north? And why, for that matter, did she think so often — too often — of that strange youngster with the pet mouse?

Time to go to bed.

She pushed her coffee cup away impatiently and walked out into the hall next to the emergency area. Her car, she remembered, was parked in the spot reserved for chief of surgery. She hurried her pace.

Busy tonight, she noted, as she picked her way through Emergency, past the rubber-wheeled stretchers lining each wall with their subdued white-gowned burdens; past the young mother with the wide, scared eyes, who kept smoothing the downy head of a baby far too pale, far too still; past a silent grey-haired man who leaned on two canes, his face the colour of dirty chalk; past a broad-backed young man in construction boots and overalls, with one arm angled oddly away from a bloodied shoulder, who stood silent amidst the rapid buttery speech of his Portuguese parents and brothers and sisters.

Nell glanced curiously at the big red-headed woman who sat just beyond them, immobile as a sculpture except for the small movements of her fingers on the heavy gold cross she wore, and the slow blink of her large blue eyes as she stared at the door of the examining room opposite. Beside her sat a boy with a tobacco tin.

Nell halted in mid-stride. "Barney!"

The young face, stained with smoke and tears, turned towards her, the deep brown eyes wary at first, then melting into gladness as he recognized her.

"Nell!" He rose and came to her. She held out her hands and he grabbed them tight. She looked at him. Trouble. Terrible trouble. She saw it in his face. She opened her mouth to speak, to ask a dozen questions, but her tongue had no time to frame the words. A shout rang through the corridor behind her.

"Stop that kid! Stop him!"

For a second, no more, Nell glimpsed the contorted face of the young policeman she had seen upstairs on Station Two. Then Harry Moss, frantic as a roped calf, barrelled into her. She stumbled backwards, trying to protect Barney, and braced her wiry body against a stretcher. Harry was stopped in his tracks. Slowly he put a hand to his head in confusion and pain, and fell forward into Nell's astonished arms.

* * *

Bill Conrad pressed harder on the gas pedal. He laughed out loud, a joyful sound in the darkness of his car. The headlights of the VW leaped southward. The phone call had come at last. Barney was safe. His son — he whispered the words — his son was safe. They had a second chance.

* * *

The hospital at midnight was hushed. Footfalls were muted, voices only a murmur. On the fifth floor, in the east wing operating room, four surgeons moved their hands in a practised magical pattern into and across the body of Michael Dennis McGee. The clank of scalpels against the stainless steel basin added tinny notes to the whispering harmony of the green uniforms, the breathing of the nurses through their masks, the doctors' monosyllables of demand, the harsh pull and gasp of the respiration monitor as it sent messages from the seared lungs.

The room crackled with urgency, an urgency the green-robed figures knew too well. They knew they must not allow it to hurry them, to blunt their skills, to destroy the fine control that might, that just might, snatch a victory from the enemy that sometimes retreated but never surrendered.

123

Mike's scrubbed, swathed body looked garish beneath the high-powered overhead lights. His face seemed remote, almost tranquil, supremely indifferent to the odd ceremonies being performed upon the rest of him. He seemed attached to life only by the fragile pipes and tubes flowing into and out of him — and by the unseen thread of hope and fear which joined him to the three who sat in the waiting room down the hall.

Barney's eyes snapped open. He glanced at the clock. One-thirty. Must've fallen asleep for a few minutes. He moved on the leather couch, wondering how he could ever have thought it comfortable. He took Saki out of the tin again and gently stroked the mouse's belly, brushing the last flecks of soot from the fine ivory fur. The little animal yawned and stretched out flat on Barney's hand, contented after nibbling on a half-dozen potato chips, ready now to forgive his companion for the strange and disagreeable night. The boy watched him, a tired grin erasing for a moment the lines of worry on his face.

Nell, observing the tableau, smiled in turn. Quite a pair, she thought. Barney had told her the whole story as they sat watching the clock make its unending circular journey, as they sat waiting for someone to come and tell them the worst. Nell's face sobered; it might indeed be the worst. She had spoken to the intern in Emergency — Mike had been admitted with extensive chest injuries, a possible ruptured spleen and second- and third-degree burns to his arms, head and back. To her questioning look, the intern had shrugged, shaken his head and turned away. Nell knew the translation: Mike McGee, a drifter, a bum, a nobody, might just possibly die.

Two-fifteen.

Nell's glance shifted to Maggie, who filled the chair in which she sat like a large and flamboyantly feathered bird brooding on a nest. Beside her Nell felt small and drab. She knew she would never forget the startling blue goodness of Maggie's eyes, eyes now shadowed with the pain of not knowing what would happen to the man who lay unconscious down the hall. The pain had given her away, Nell reflected. For Maggie saw a Mike the world didn't see, she knew a Mike the world didn't know; she looked beyond the man he was to the man he might have been and could perhaps still be, and to that man she was bound. If Mike lived, thought Nell, he would be doubly lucky.

Three o'clock.

With sudden restless fingers Nell crushed the styrofoam cup which had held her fourth coffee and moved to the window. Her mind wandered briefly to the lonely figure of Harry Moss, the feel of his thin trembling body a few hours ago in Emergency, the look in his eyes. The boy had no one. No one wanted him. She knew the feeling.

She knew she could help. Her pulse quickened a little as she began to arrange in her mind the practical steps to be taken: the police, the courts, the youth bureau, legal aid, maybe probation. And counselling. There was a lot she could do for Harry, a lot. If he would let her.

She glanced downwards and saw a Volkswagen hurtle around the corner and into the broad driveway. It jolted to a halt in a *NO PARKING* zone. A man unfolded himself from the little car and strode rapidly towards the entrance, disappearing from view beneath the canopy.

A noise made her turn. She saw Maggie and Barney staring at the doorway. Dr. Alger, his green mask dangling, his face marked with four hours of effort, stood there uncertainly. "McGee?" His voice rose questioningly.

Barney stood up like a jack-in-the-box. His hand reached convulsively for Maggie's. Fear crouched in his stomach, ready to spring. And the guilt, the terrible guilt he had borne these long hours, the feeling that in some way the nightmare had been his fault, pressed inside his head until he felt dizzy.

"I'm Barney McGee, sir," he whispered. "Mike McGee's my father."

Dr. Alger's face creased stiffly into a tired smile. He gripped the boy's shoulder. "Well, Barney, your father made it. He'll be a long time getting better, but we think he's going to be all right."

Barney couldn't stop his mouth from shaking. The muscles in his legs began to tremble and give way. He sat down quickly before he fell, still clutching Maggie's hand. He started to cry, and lowering his head to hide the tears, did not see the tall man with horn-rimmed glasses stop in the doorway, did not see, as did Nell, how the

126

man's face lit when he saw Barney, how the man's hands lifted towards the boy for a moment before they dropped and curved tensely at his sides.

Nell crossed the room. "Mr. Conrad?" At his nod she continued, her voice low. "I'm Nell Weatherston, a social worker here. I know your stepson and why he's here." She smiled to put the man at ease and quickly sketched in the details of the evening. "And Mr. Conrad, if I could make a suggestion" — she glanced at him keenly, then, satisfied, went on — "go easy. Don't press."

Bill Conrad returned her look and nodded slowly. He hesitated, then moved forward until he stood in front of Maggie and Barney.

"Barney." His voice was warm and low.

Startled, the boy looked up. He snatched his hand from Maggie's and rubbed at the tears on his face.

Bill Conrad took a step towards him and said, "That's okay, Barney." There was a silence. "How are you? How's Saki?" He put a gentle forefinger on the mouse, now curled on Barney's shoulder.

"Okay. We're both okay." His voice was just a whisper.

"Is it all right if I sit with you for a while?"

"Oh, sure." The boy shifted on the couch to make room. "Uh, Maggie, this is my — my stepfather. From up north." He turned in Conrad's direction but avoided meeting his glance. "This is Maggie. She's a friend of Mike's."

"I'm pleased to meet you, Maggie." Conrad offered his hand.

Barney looked at his boots, counting the holes where the dirty laces wove in and out. He cleared his throat. Then he cleared it again. He was sure having trouble talking, he thought.

Finally he said, "How's Mom?" His voice sounded queer in his own ears. And his throat felt as if it had a bunch of rocks in it.

"She's fine." Conrad paused, then said, almost under his breath, unable to help himself, "Now."

Barney flashed him a look, then stared at his boots again. After a long time he whispered, "I'm sorry if I got her worried. I didn't mean things to turn out this way."

"I know." Conrad pushed his hands into his jacket pockets and nervously pulled them out again. "She asked me to ask you to come home, Barney." His voice trembled a little.

The rocks in Barney's throat got bigger. He said nothing, just turned his head to look at the man beside him. Bill Conrad met his look squarely, gravely, humbly, and said, "And I want you to come home too, Barney. Will you?"

Barney couldn't answer. He looked across at Nell. She was smiling. He looked at Maggie. She leaned forward and patted his knee. Finally he turned to his stepfather and slowly nodded his head.

As good as new

The room was cool and dim, with a faint antiseptic tang. Barney stood by the side of the bed. The morning sunlight glinted on the upside-down plastic bag of intravenous fluid which dripped slow nourishment into his father's bandaged arm. Tubes ran from his nose; the flesh surrounding them was red and blistered. His body seemed small and shrunken and vulnerable there in the big bed. Barney had a sudden painful sense that Mike was the child and he the father. He blinked at the strangeness of it.

Mike's eyes fluttered a little, then opened halfway. It was a moment before he focused on the waiting boy. He moved his lips but no sound came out. Barney leaned closer. Mike's mouth worked again. "Hi, Barn."

"Hi. Don't talk, Mike." For a split second a question skipped across the surface of Barney's mind: why had he never called this man Dad?

"How's — how's the little mouse?" A smile tried to form on the swollen lips.

"He's fine, Mike. Thanks to you."

"Good." Mike's eyes closed and his head slipped to one side. Barney didn't know what to do. He stood there for what seemed a long time, then whispered, "You asleep, Mike?"

The reply was slow. "Restin', Barn. Tired." A frown appeared on Mike's face and his eyes jerked open. With a burst of energy he raised himself a little from the bed and looked directly at Barney.

"Go home, son. You don't belong here. It's no good for you here." His voice was a scraping whisper.

"But Mike, I — "

"Don't argue with your old man, boy." A crooked smile erased the harshness of the words. "Believe me, I know what's good for you." He sank back and turned his face away so that Barney caught only a few of his next words: ". . . why I left . . . ten years ago . . . give you . . . chance."

Barney stood there, awkward, silent. He could think of nothing to say. But he felt as if a great weight had been lifted from him. And he knew that Mike was right. He had known it before Mike had said it. He couldn't stay. He touched his father's fingers lightly.

"I'll come to visit, Mike. I'll — I'll come down to see you."

"Sure, Barn." Mike's voice had sunk to a quavering murmur. "Maggie'll write you. When I'm better." His eyes closed. "You do that, Barn. Yeah."

"I will, Mike, I really will. And you'll be better before you know it, I bet!" He forced himself to sound cheerful, despite the shaking in his stomach. Then he leaned down and kissed the worn cheek. " 'Bye, Mike. I'll see you."

130

Barney stumbled from the room, not seeing the odd smile, half pain, half contentment, that for a moment gave his father's face a kind of dignity.

* * *

Harry didn't turn his head when the door opened. For one thing, he didn't care any more who came to see him. It didn't really matter if it were the Prime Minister or the Holy Ghost, he'd had it now. He'd get sent away for sure. And nobody would give a damn, nobody in the whole world.

For another thing, it hurt too much. Every time he moved, his head ached worse, and he got so dizzy it just about made him sick. Even when he was lying flat on his back like now. Ever since he'd run into that lady with the grey hair. It was her fault. If she hadn't been in the way . . .

Then he heard her voice saying his name.

* * *

The highway unrolled beneath them like a shiny black measuring tape. Barney watched it, silent, half-hypnotized, sometimes falling into a kind of dream, stirring only briefly when his stepfather pulled out to pass a tractor or a load of hay. Only the rush of wind and the muffled rhythm of the engine were audible.

Barney could sense Conrad looking at him every now and then, but he kept his eyes straight ahead. He was more tired than he'd ever been in his life. And he felt all mixed up. So much had happened. He touched Saki, bedded in his pocket, and was comforted by the mouse's nearness and warmth.

Once he broke the silence. "He saved Saki, you know; Mike saved Saki."

Bill Conrad gave him a swift glance then turned his eyes back to the road. "I know, Barney," he said quietly. "it was a brave thing to do."

"Yes," said Barney. "That's something, anyway." Then he added, almost to himself, "Nobody can take that away from him."

They fell silent again. Just north of Benedict Barney drifted into an uneasy sleep, until the harsh squeal of brakes jolted him awake. His chest was jammed against the safety belt. Ahead of them a groundhog ambled across the highway, deaf to the screaming tires, bent only on reaching his burrow in the neighbouring cornfield. The sunlight glinted on the reddish fur of the animal's shoulders and forelegs. Conrad swerved the VW sharply left, then straightened it out.

Still blurry with sleep, Barney mumbled, *"Marmota monax rufescens."*

Bill Conrad blinked in surprise, then grinned. He started to chuckle. "You still remember?"

Barney turned and smiled. "Sure." Then he laughed too.

They passed the sign that read *CHESSBOROUGH SPEED LIMIT 50 kmh EXCEPT WHERE OTHERWISE POSTED.* Landmarks flowed by. Barney felt as if he'd been away for a year. Everything seemed strange, yet warmly familiar. City Hall, the post office, the shopping plaza, the marina, even the empty schoolyard spoke to him in welcoming whispers of memory.

He was home, he thought. This was home, all this. The places he had grown up in, the town he knew end to end, the hills behind it, the rocks, the trees, the lakes and streams he and Mr. Conrad had found together. Guess I'll have to stop calling him mister, Barney thought.

Mike had been right. He couldn't have stayed in Toronto. He couldn't have stayed even if there hadn't been a fire, even if Mike hadn't been hurt. The laughing young man who had seemed to beckon to him from the old photograph, who had seemed to promise him adventure and freedom, didn't exist. Maybe he had never existed, except in Barney's mind. Maybe he had made Mike up because he wanted to run away. The way Mike had run away ten years before. It doesn't work, Barney thought; running away just doesn't work. All you get is a whole new set of problems, some of them tougher than the ones you had before. Maybe being free was something else altogether. He'd have to think about it later on, try to sort it out.

They passed the street where Dave lived. Barney wondered how Dave was, and his heart beat a little faster. It sure would be great to see Dave again. Man, wait till Dave heard what had happened!

Then they were turning into the rough gravel driveway of the old house. It looked the same as before: it needed paint, the shutters were loose, and the brick chimney had a dangerous tilt. But to Barney it looked just fine. Before his stepfather had turned off the ignition he was out of the car and running up the steps. The door was flung open as he touched the knob and he was enveloped in his mother's arms. He hugged her as tight as he could. And she hugged him back, laughing and crying at the same time, saying his name over and over.

Conrad watched, a smile spreading over his features and brightening his eyes. Finally, when the welcome was done, he said, "Well! How about some tea? Do you want to make it, Barney? I'll get the cups."

Barney moved to the kitchen and reached into the cupboard. When his hand fell on the teapot, he stopped for a moment in surprise. Behind him Conrad said, "It's safe to use, Barney. I fixed it."

Cautiously Barney took the blue and white teapot in his two hands. He looked at the spout. It seemed okay. Just like new.

Bill Conrad moved closer, until their heads almost touched. "See, Barn? If you really look hard you can see where it's mended."

Barney squinted. There was a tiny vein-like line circling the spout. "Yeah. I see it."

Conrad hesitated a moment, then continued softly. "Barney, sometimes when things get broken and then put back together, they're even stronger than before. Do you believe that?"

Barney looked up. "I think so." His voice was low. "I want to believe it, Mr. — I mean — Dad."

For an instant the man's face was serious and still. Then he started to smile. Barney smiled back.

134

All of a sudden he felt better than he had in a long, long time.

He reached for the tea.